FOR BETTER OR FOR WORSE

THE VOWS BOOK 2

HEIDI RENEE MASON

BOOKS

Always Hope (stand alone)
Love At First Crepe (Sweet Escape 1)
Just Double the Recipe (Sweet Escape 2)
To Have and To Hold (The Vows 1)
For Better or For Worse (The Vows 2)
'Til Death Do Us Part (The Vows 3)
Nothing Hidden Even Stays (Writing as HR Mason)

For information, contact the publisher, Hot Tree Publishing.

www.hottreepublishing.com

Editing: Hot Tree Editing

Cover Designer: Soxsational Cover Design

ISBN: 978-1-925853-76-6

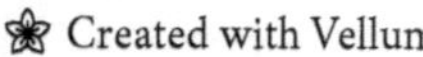 Created with Vellum

This book is dedicated to my three daughters and women everywhere. You are stronger than you know. Be your own hero.

ONE

PANIC ROSE INSIDE OF HER. HER STOMACH CHURNED WITH DREAD. *Xavier had Emma securely tethered to the kitchen chair. The zip ties cut into her flesh, and the blood dripped from the cut on her lip and pooled on her chest.*

He paced back and forth wildly, like a tiger in a cage. With her hands and feet bound, she was helpless. He came to a stop and stood in front of her, his face only inches away from her own. The insanity was obvious behind his steel-gray eyes.

"Where are the jewels, Emma?" Xavier raised his voice in anger. "Don't tell me you don't know where they are."

"The jewels?" She did her best to focus on what she needed to do to get out of the situation. She tried to slow her pounding heart, but her attempts were futile. She was in full-blown panic mode.

Without warning, Xavier punched her in the face. Her head snapped back from the force and blood ran down her chin. He hit her again, singularly focused on hurting her. The kindness she'd observed earlier was gone. There was nothing human behind his vacant eyes. The man had disappeared; in his place was a monster.

Her time was running out if she didn't do something, so she used the only tool at her disposal. She opened her mouth and screamed loudly, a blood-curdling scream that she hoped someone would hear. She yelled until her lungs were on fire, as she prayed that someone would come to her rescue.

Suddenly, the shattering sound of glass echoed in the quiet of the house. The last thing she saw before she lost consciousness was Liam.

"Emma, honey, wake up. You're dreaming, baby. I'm right here. You're okay." Liam wrapped his strong arms around his wife and whispered soothing words that eventually brought her back to the present.

Emma opened her eyes and tried to push down the terror. She was okay. She was in her bed, with her husband.

She took several deep, calming breaths and willed herself to forget the dream.

"Sorry." She was ashamed that her nightmares had continued with such regularity over the past four months. No matter how hard she tried, she couldn't shake them.

"Emma, stop apologizing. It's not your fault. Dr. Woods said nightmares are perfectly normal after a traumatic event. It's only been four months since Xavier broke into the house and attacked you. You can't expect to just forget what he did to you."

Liam clenched his teeth, and she could almost feel the anger he harbored inside. He blamed himself for not being able to prevent the incident. No matter how many times she told him it wasn't his fault, he couldn't accept it. They both had a long way to go on the road to recovery.

Other than the nightmares, the last four months had been the happiest of her life. Theirs was a whirlwind romance, but she wouldn't change a thing if it meant they ended up together. They'd had some logistical details to manage, but they'd done just fine. Liam had sold his house, and they were both happy to be rid of it. Living there was out of the question. Not only had it been the house where her husband's mistress, Veronica Smith, lived and stashed billions of dollars' worth of stolen jewels, but it was also next door to the house where Jacob and Emma had spent their unhappy marriage. Rosemary Lane held too many bad memories, and she was more than happy to close that chapter of her life.

Instead, Liam moved into Emma's house, the large Victorian home her parents left her when they died. It was like a house out of a storybook, big and cozy with more than enough room for everyone. It was an added bonus that it also boasted an upstairs apartment where her best friend, Sadie Ross, lived. It was the perfect place to raise their growing family.

Emma and Liam had a small, private wedding ceremony only days after her release from the hospital. When she'd learned she was pregnant with Liam's child in the emergency room after her brutal attack, she had known they were meant to be together. Her pregnancy had ultimately brought the estranged couple back together.

When she found out Liam was the FBI agent who was secretly investigating her deceased husband, she'd wanted nothing more to do with him. She'd felt betrayed because he hadn't been up front with her from the start. Finding out that they were going to have a baby was the reminder she needed to show her what was really important in life.

Liam's family had flown in from Chicago for the wedding. After meeting them, she could clearly see why her husband loved them so much. His parents, Duncan and Eliza, were amazing, and so was his sister, Leslie, her husband, Tom, and their daughters, Amber and Alicia. They'd welcomed her and her three daughters with open arms.

It was nice to have that family connection in her life once

again. She hadn't realized how much she craved it. Of course, she missed her own parents desperately, and no one could ever replace them, but having Liam's family was an amazing gift, and she'd come to cherish them. They had all settled into their new lives happily and comfortably.

She stretched out in bed and tried to chase away the stressful feelings that always lingered after the nightmares ended. Emma hated that Xavier was still a part of her life. She wanted nothing more than to forget about the attack and move on, but that was wishful thinking; Xavier still haunted her thoughts and invaded her dreams every single night. Even though she knew he was in prison and couldn't hurt her, she still wasn't able to get past the trauma.

A wave of nausea rolled through her body, and she breathed in slowly through her nose and out through her mouth until it passed. Some days it didn't pass. She was hungry, but the churning of her stomach suggested food was not the best idea. At six months pregnant, she was still experiencing morning sickness. Her fourth pregnancy was shaping up to be quite different than her previous three.

In the beginning, the differences had convinced her that she was carrying a boy. However, the ultrasound during the second trimester had disproved that theory. The expectant parents were expecting girl number four. Continuing the flower theme, they decided the name Daisy went well with Lily, Rose, and Dahlia.

When they'd found out it was another girl, Emma expected Liam to be a little bit disappointed. After all, every man wanted a boy to carry on his name. Surprisingly, Liam couldn't have been happier upon finding out that another female would be joining his brood. Secretly, Emma was also relieved. She knew what to do with girls, and she couldn't really picture herself as the mom of a little boy. Girls were her thing, and soon she would have four of them.

Rose's running feet pounded down the hallway. She'd turned seven last month, and she was always the first one to wake each morning. Emma wished she could take her youngest daughter's energy and bottle it. In the O'Reilly house, a lazy Saturday morning was nothing more than a fantasy.

Rose jumped on the bed between her parents and promptly asked for food. "My tummy woke me up, it was rumbling so much," she groaned as if she hadn't eaten in weeks.

"Well, I guess I'd better fix you some food before you waste away to nothing!" Emma planted a kiss on Rose's head and rolled over slowly.

Her baby bump had become large much sooner with the fourth pregnancy, and movement was becoming increasingly more difficult. Jumping out of bed quickly was a thing of the past.

"Let's let Mama wake up slowly, Rosie. Get your sisters, and I'll fix breakfast for you." Liam hopped out of bed and threw on a sweatshirt.

"I'll go get them, Daddy!" Rose ran down the hall screaming her sisters' names.

It warmed Emma's heart to hear her daughters call Liam "Daddy." The minute they'd told the girls they were getting married, they'd asked Liam to adopt them. Their father, Jacob, had been dead for over seven years, and Lily and Dahlia barely remembered him. Rose had never even met him. Liam filled that vacant space they had inside. It wasn't something they'd forced; it had all happened organically. Liam was beyond thrilled with his new parental role, and Emma was happy that their family was complete. Next month, the adoption would be final, and the girls would legally belong to Liam.

A swift kick to her rib cage let her know that the littlest

member of the family was up and about. Daisy took great joy in pushing on her mother's bladder, especially first thing in the morning.

Emma rolled out of bed gingerly and headed to the bathroom. It was time to begin a new day.

TWO

Emma stood in the shower and let the hot water work on all her aches and pains. Her current pregnancy was vastly different from the prior three. Perhaps it was because she was older than she'd been with her other pregnancies. She'd been in her early twenties then. This time, her body hurt constantly, she was exhausted, and her energy level was nonexistent. She tried her best not to let it show, but some days were easier than others. Between running her coffee shop and caring for her family, she didn't have time to take it easy. Her life was a hurricane that continuously gained momentum.

She turned off the water, stepped out of the shower, and took a look at herself in the mirror, frowning as she made note of the changes in her body. Not thin to begin with, she'd already gained more weight than she wanted, and she felt unattractive and awkward. Liam assured her every day that he thought she was beautiful, but she'd become overly critical of what she saw in her reflection. She knew her body would return to normal after she gave birth, but that seemed very far away.

Sighing, she headed to her room to get dressed. She threw on black leggings and a green tunic, combed out her long strawberry-blonde hair, applied minimal makeup, and headed downstairs. Liam had managed to wrangle all three girls to the kitchen table, where they were feasting on pancakes and fruit. He was an amazing man, and he always jumped in to lighten the load when she needed him to, which seemed to be often.

"Morning, Mama." Nine-year-old Dahlia smiled at her mother as she kissed the child's blonde head.

She had one mood, and it was perpetual happiness. The little girl's blue eyes exuded kindness, and if ever there were a perfect child, she was it. Unfortunately Dahlia's sisters weren't quite as low-maintenance.

"Morning, Dahlia. I like the way you fixed your hair today." Emma smiled at her middle child before acknowledging her oldest. "You also look very cute this morning, Lily."

Lily had an intense aversion to mornings. Rather than being granted a happy smile for the compliment, Emma received a scowl instead. In typical Lily fashion, the girl grunted and tossed her reddish-blonde hair as if she were in a shampoo commercial. Emma took a deep breath and reminded herself to remain patient.

"Thanks for waking your sisters for me, Rose. Looks like Dad made yummy pancakes. Did you all say thank you?"

Liam handed his wife a perfectly prepared breakfast plate. "Yes, they thanked me." He smiled at her and she kissed him on the cheek.

"So, what do you guys want to do today? Jane is working all day at Morning Glory, so I don't have to go in. Dad has the day off too. We should do something fun." Emma sat at the kitchen table and took a gigantic bite of pancakes. Her stomach was much less queasy, and she felt like she could eat ten of them.

"I think we should drive to Warfield and go to the mall. I need new clothes." Lily, who had been scowling only a moment ago, perked right up as she suggested a shopping trip.

Lily acted more like a teenager than an eleven-year-old. Her idea of fun usually revolved around adding to her wardrobe. Emma couldn't imagine what life would be like when she actually was a teenager. Her mood swings gave her mother whiplash already.

"I don't really want to go to the mall. We should see a movie." Dahlia would be happy going through life in her pajamas, so she never volunteered to go shopping.

"I want new clothes and a movie," Rose piped up, her mouth filled with pancakes. Emma gave her a disapproving look. The little girl closed her mouth and continued to chew.

"Well, why don't we drive to the Warfield Mall. We can do some shopping and then see a movie?" Liam responded diplomatically. He was getting the hang of being surrounded by women.

"Good idea. I have some things to do around the house, so let's go this afternoon. I could use some new clothes since I'm growing out of everything I own." Emma frowned and shoveled more pancakes into her mouth.

"You are the most beautiful woman I've ever seen." He grinned as he cleared the dirty dishes from the table.

"You're supposed to say that," Emma huffed.

"I don't say things I don't mean. You are beautiful." He leaned down and kissed the top of her head.

Emma's heart fluttered inside of her chest, and it felt as if a thousand butterflies were set free. The chemistry between the two of them was still going strong. She'd worried that marriage would change their dynamic, but so far, it wasn't the case. She still had a physical reaction to Liam every time he was near. Their bond was powerful, and if anything, marriage had made it even stronger. She hoped that never changed. She'd experienced the monotony of marriage before, and she didn't want that for them.

She finished eating and loaded her plate into the dishwasher. Liam had already cleaned the rest of the kitchen, so there was little left to do. The man was like a machine, and she couldn't seem to keep up with him.

"Girls, go upstairs and get dressed. Straighten up your rooms, and we will go in a bit," she instructed her daughters.

She contemplated asking Sadie to go along, but then she remembered her friend was working. As the town's research librarian, her schedule could be hectic at certain times of the year. She'd been so busy lately. Even though she lived upstairs, they hadn't been able to carve away any time together in weeks. She missed her best friend.

A few hours later they packed into the SUV, ready to make the forty-five-minute trip to Warfield. Beckland was the perfect idyllic small town, which meant the closest mall was in the next county. Emma didn't mind the drive at all, as Ohio was beautiful in the fall.

It was mid-October, and nature's scenery was like a painting. Leaves of scarlet and gold adorned the treetops. Soon those leaves would fall to the ground, and her children would take pleasure in jumping in the piles. The air was crisp and invigorating, bringing to mind images of pumpkins and hay rides. Unfortunately, it also made her think of coffee, which she'd given up the day she discovered she was pregnant with Daisy.

Even though her doctor made assurances that one cup of caffeine each day was perfectly safe, she wasn't willing to take the chance. As she'd done every time, she took certain precautions when she was pregnant. She told herself that the coffee would taste even better when she was able to have it again. She looked forward to her first sip of caffeinated goodness as soon as she gave birth.

Emma glanced at Liam as he drove. His black hair curled around his ears, and she wanted to reach out and twirl it around her finger. Instead, she clasped his hand in hers. He smiled and squeezed her hand as their fingers intertwined. He seemed quiet, withdrawn, and in a state of deep concentration. He was probably focused on work.

As an FBI agent, Liam never really "turned off" the job. Dedication was a large part of his core values, and one of many things Emma admired about her husband. The cases he investigated weighed heavily on him. She often wondered how he dealt with such a stressful occupation as well as he did. In contrast, Emma knew she would be a basket case if she had to see even half of the things he'd seen.

The girls were uncharacteristically quiet in the back seat, and she almost forgot they were in the car. She turned around and saw Dahlia was reading, and Rose and Lily were playing a game on the iPad. Everyone seemed to be enjoying the ride, even if they weren't sharing her appreciation of the lovely scenery.

Forty-five minutes later, they pulled into the parking lot of the Warfield Mall. It was packed, so Emma and the girls piled out of the SUV and went inside while Liam circled the lot twice before finally finding a space.

The mall was a hubbub of activity, full of shoppers scurrying in search of the perfect item. Emma and her family navigated the crowd, carefully keeping an eye on Rose, who liked to wander. A mother's worst fear was losing one of her children in a sea of strangers.

They shopped their favorite stores, making a few purchases along the way. It seemed that every time Emma turned around, her daughters had grown out of their clothes.

They purchased several new fall outfits, and even picked up winter coats for each girl, since last year's would no longer fit.

The girls were hungry and cranky, so Liam took them and all the bags to scope out the food court while she browsed the maternity section at her favorite boutique. She selected several new shirts, a pair of maternity jeans, three tunics, and new black leggings. Happy with her purchases, she jumped on the escalator and went to find her family.

When she reached the mall's lower level, she stepped off the moving stairs, careful not to lose her balance, and headed toward the food court. She was thinking about the cute clothes she'd just purchased and wasn't really paying attention to where she was going. Before she knew what was happening, she collided with a woman who was barreling her way, almost as if she were aiming for Emma.

The women bumped into one another, and the impact nearly caused Emma to topple over. She managed to catch herself and somehow didn't fall. She wasn't agile on her best days, but at six months pregnant, she was more than a little bit clumsy. She looked around to see if anyone in the crowd had noticed the occurrence. The shoppers continued about their business, blissfully oblivious. Emma just stood there in shock, trying to figure out why the woman had plowed into her with such force. It wasn't as if she was difficult to notice.

"I'm sorry. Excuse me," Emma said, trying to regain her composure.

"You're an ignorant cow! Why don't you watch where you're going? You walked right into me!" The woman, a stunning, model-thin, dark-haired beauty, raised her voice in anger.

Emma was shocked at her reaction. She couldn't believe the woman was yelling at her when she'd clearly been responsible for their collision.

"It's not necessary to call me names. In case you didn't notice, you're the one who slammed into me." Emma's voice trembled with anger as she tried hard to keep her temper under control.

"You weren't paying attention to where you were going. You should have been watching. You should have gotten out of my way!" the woman continued to yell loudly.

Before long, her raised voice drew a crowd of curious shoppers who came to check out the commotion. Emma observed the stranger before her. They were about the same age, and she had long chocolate-brown hair so shiny that it looked like glass. The woman had piercing blue eyes, and she was remarkably beautiful. She was also looking at Emma as if she wanted to kill her.

"Listen, I didn't mean to bump into you, but you look just fine to me. You're not hurt, are you?" Emma asked incredulously.

She couldn't believe the stranger was making such a big deal out of nothing. After all, if anyone had the right to be mad, it was Emma.

"Lady, if you know what's good for you, you'll watch your back. One of these days you're going to get what's coming to you," the woman spat as she stomped away. The crowd parted to let her pass.

Emma shook her head in disbelief as her heart continued to pound. She hated confrontations, and that one had been totally unexpected. She couldn't believe the woman had threatened her over an accidental collision. She'd blown the entire event out of proportion.

An uneasy feeling settled inside, but she forced herself to calm down. Ignoring the crowd who continued to gawk, she walked quickly toward the food court to find her family.

THREE

After having dinner at the mall, they took the girls to see a movie. As with most shows that she'd watched in the last eleven years, it was full of princesses and singing animals.

They stuffed themselves with popcorn and gummy bears, and when the movie was over, they headed home. The ride seemed long, and by the time they finally pulled into the driveway, the girls were sound asleep in the back seat, using each other's shoulders for headrests. It was so sweet, and she was tempted to snap a picture, but she didn't want to wake them. Liam carried the girls, one by one, up the winding staircase to their beds. Prowling the mall had clearly worn them out.

"Only one more to go, and then we can collapse into bed too," Liam whispered as he gently lifted Rose out of the car and carried her upstairs.

"That sounds like a dream come true to my feet right now," Emma answered quietly.

She hadn't told him about the disturbing confrontation with the stranger, but it had been gnawing at her all afternoon. The intensity of the woman's anger still rankled. At the time, Emma had been angry, but she'd been afraid of the woman as well. Something about the exchange was off, but she didn't know why. The woman's fury seemed disproportionate to the event.

Knowing she would never see the woman again, Emma told herself to forget it. She had enough stress in her life, and she didn't need to add more. Her wise mother had always said, "Don't borrow trouble," which was exactly what she was doing by worrying about something that was over.

She went upstairs to prepare for bed. The familiar sight of her down comforter and fluffy pillows was a welcome vision to her tired, pregnant, aching body. She could not get there soon enough.

She went into the bathroom to put on pajamas. As she undressed, a quick glance in the mirror showed the beginnings of a very large bruise on her arm. Bruises weren't an unfamiliar sight to Emma, especially in her clumsier-than-usual pregnant state, but that one was large and very tender, and she tried to think of what might have caused it.

As she examined the black-and-blue mark, it came to her. It was caused by the collision with the woman at the mall. At the time, she'd been so focused on the argument that she hadn't even noticed she'd been hurt. Between anger and adrenaline, she hadn't paid attention to anything else. She placed her hand on the spot on her arm and realized it was painful. The crazy woman had hit her hard. Emma was sure she had taken the brunt of the hit. For someone so small, the stranger packed a punch.

She rubbed arnica on the bruise and hoped Liam wouldn't notice. He was even more protective since she'd become pregnant. He would blame himself for not being there to stop it. While she appreciated his concern, sometimes he went overboard. If he saw the gigantic bruise, it would be one of those times.

Once her bedtime chores were finished, she allowed herself to collapse into bed. Liam followed soon after. They held each other in the darkness and the events of the day ceased to be important. She thought of how blessed they were. They had three amazing daughters, another one on the way, careers they loved, and wonderful family and friends. They also had each other. Emma couldn't imagine what her life would look like if Liam had never walked into her coffee shop. She'd been reluctant to give him a chance, but she was so glad he hadn't given up on her.

Before Liam, her life had been fine, but she was lonely. She was guarded and distrusting, but Liam's love and acceptance had changed her. He opened her heart, and she was able to see how closed-off she really was. Her first marriage had been a disaster. She'd married her high school sweetheart and settled into a comfortable life, but there was no passion. Only after Jacob was killed in a plane crash with his mistress did she find out that he'd been unfaithful to her for years. The heartache that resulted from that discovery was more than she could bear, so she withdrew from nearly everyone.

After her parents were killed in a car accident, she began to believe that life was out to get her. Liam made her understand that it was important to trust others and allow herself to be vulnerable. She was even learning to be optimistic and trying hard not to believe that trouble was lurking around every corner.

Meeting Liam had changed her life. In the span of a few months, they met and fell in love. Then she discovered that Liam was investigating Veronica and Jacob for stealing billions of dollars' worth of jewels. That was a tough pill to swallow. She realized she'd never known her ex-husband at all, and she was angry with Liam for not being honest about his part in the situation. Just when she believed things couldn't get more complicated, she was attacked in her home by Veronica's jealous ex-husband, she was rescued, she discovered she was pregnant, and then she and Liam were married. All of these were huge, monumental, life-altering events. Emma's boring, steady, predictable life was practically unrecognizable.

Liam's breathing became slow and steady, and she knew he was asleep. How she wished sleep came that easily for her. Lately, slumber was something elusive, always waiting just outside of her grasp. She was exhausted, and she wanted nothing more than to close her eyes and slip into glorious oblivion, but as tired as she was, she was terrified to close her eyes. Instead of peaceful rest, her sleeping hours had become plagued with terror.

Even though her rational mind knew she was safe in her house, lying next to her husband who would die to protect her, Emma was afraid to go to sleep. As much as he wanted to, Liam couldn't keep her safe from the horrors of her own mind. Every night it was the same. Xavier was there, waiting for her in her dreams.

FOUR

Sunday was family day in the O'Reilly house. Liam and Emma kept their schedules open and always spent the day with the girls. They had a quick breakfast at home before heading off to church. After services, they went to The Railroad, a local diner, for brunch.

She had introduced the tradition of Sunday brunch at The Railroad a few months ago. Emma's parents had always taken her there after church when she was growing up. Fostering traditions was important, and The Railroad was one of her favorites. Not only was it something special for her to share with the girls, but it gave her an excuse not to cook on Sunday afternoons. Between work, pregnancy, keeping up with her family, and her recent lack of sleep, she was happy to take cooking off her list.

After brunch, the family went home and spent the rest of the day relaxing. Lazy Sundays carried Emma through the rest of her busy week; they allowed her to decompress and prepare both mentally and physically for the week ahead. Liam settled in to watch a football game, the girls played with their dolls, and she flopped into bed for a quick rest that somehow turned into a two-hour nap.

When she woke and headed downstairs, she discovered Liam had already started dinner. He was pulling more than his fair share of the weight around the house, and she chided herself. She needed to get her act together and stop relying on him to do everything. He worked hard too, and he shouldn't be responsible for taking care of their shared chores alone while she slept the day away. There was a time when she'd been energetic enough to do it all, but those days were over.

"Hey, sleepyhead." Liam smiled as she entered the kitchen.

The sun had come out while she was asleep, and its rays were streaming cheerfully through the large bay window. Sunbeams danced on the yellow walls, and the light made a rainbow as it glinted off the antique crystal chandelier that hung over the table. The kitchen, which Emma's mother had decorated many years ago, was exactly the same as it had been when she was a little girl. The feeling of continuity soothed her. The kitchen was the room where she felt her mother's presence the strongest.

"Sorry I slept so long. I just meant to close my eyes for a few minutes." Embarrassment gnawed at her.

"Why are you apologizing? Don't be ridiculous. You're making a human being. You need the rest. Besides, you didn't miss much, other than the football game. I recorded it for you in case you want to watch it later." Liam gave her a crooked smile that she adored.

Liam's love and Emma's dislike of football was a running joke in the O'Reilly household. Emma didn't mind if he watched it, as long as he didn't expect that she would be involved in the process. Football made no sense to her, and no matter how many times Liam tried to explain it, he might as well have been speaking a foreign language.

"It was so nice of you to record it for me, babe. You know how I love football," Emma replied sarcastically and rolled her eyes.

"Dinner will be ready in a few minutes. I made grilled chicken salads. The girls are upstairs cleaning up their mess. Every doll in the house was out earlier. It was like a Barbie invasion." Liam expertly chopped vegetables for the salad, and the chicken was already cooked. There wasn't much left for her to do.

"Thanks for taking over this afternoon. I guess I was pretty tired. My sleepless nights are catching up to me." Emma didn't like to talk about her dreams, with Liam or anyone else. Admitting Xavier still had a hold on her made her feel like a failure.

"It'll get better. I promise." Liam engulfed her in his arms. He tried so hard to make her feel safe, but she didn't.

Xavier was in prison, and she knew he couldn't hurt her. She knew fear was a funny thing—completely irrational. In the middle of the night, when the dreams came, it was real. She was terrified, and no one could protect her, not even Liam. Every night, she relived the attack all over again.

Emma knew she should talk to a counselor, but she couldn't bring herself to do it. She couldn't imagine sitting in a strange room with a head doctor while she talked about her deepest fears. Saying it out loud might make it even more real. It was better to just ignore it.

She dragged her mind away from her problems, grabbed the plates and silverware from the cupboard, and began to set the table. Liam finished dinner and then called the girls down to eat. They cleaned their plates and asked for seconds.

Emma's belly wasn't the only thing growing. Her girls were maturing every single day. Lily had the look of a young woman, right on the cusp of maturity. Sometimes she would catch a glimpse of the adults her daughters would become, and she wasn't ready for it. Dahlia's feet had grown two sizes in the last year, and her pants were all becoming too short. Rose, Emma's baby girl, was losing the baby look. Gone were the chubby cheeks and pudgy hands.

Her daughters were changing right before her eyes, and while it was the natural progression of life, it made her sad. Before long, there would be another little girl in the family who would also grow too quickly. Until she'd become a mother, she had no idea that it was possible to love another human being so strongly. It was like having your heart so full that you thought it might actually burst.

Liam and Emma cleaned the kitchen while the girls got ready for bed. She insisted that she would take care of the mess on her own, but he refused to sit down. He was such a stubborn man, but she loved him. At eight thirty, they tucked in the children, kissed them good night, and wished them sweet dreams.

When the house was finally quiet, the couple flopped onto the broken-in leather couch to watch some television. Liam gave in to his wife's pleas and turned on a chick flick. When it ended, he reluctantly admitted to her that he'd enjoyed it. Although he always insisted that he didn't like the movies she chose, Emma knew he was a sucker for a good love story.

Emma yawned and stretched, surprised that she was still tired in spite of her afternoon nap. Liam rubbed her shoulders, gently kneading her skin, and the tension began to work its way out of her muscles. She hadn't even realized she was tense, but Liam had. He worked his magic on her shoulders and neck, and then he moved to her lower back. Her body practically melted into his. His fingers moved to her scalp and he circled them in slow, rhythmic strokes.

He tilted her head back and brushed her lips with gentle kisses. Liam's lips on hers made the world fade away. It wasn't long before the gentleness turned to heat, and Emma pulled him closer. When she looked into his sea-blue eyes, she felt herself drowning.

In one smooth motion, Liam stood to his feet and lifted her into his arms. He never broke eye contact.

"Mrs. O'Reilly, I think it's time I got you to bed," he said seductively.

With a mischievous grin, he carried her upstairs.

FIVE

"NO! STOP! PLEASE DON'T HURT ME!" EMMA THRASHED IN BED beside Liam as the nightmare raged on.

"Emma, honey, wake up. You're okay." Liam gathered her trembling body into his strong arms and murmured soothing words until the dream released her from its clutches.

She opened her eyes and the sunlight streamed through the curtains. It was Monday morning, and she was safe inside of her house. She sat up in bed, trying to still the fierce beating of her heart. A surge of anger erupted as she remembered being assaulted all over again in her dreams. Xavier had control of her mind when she was awake, and he had control of her body when she was asleep. She just wanted it to stop.

"This is getting really old. I'm sick of it," she said through clenched teeth.

She was fed up with the nightmares, and she knew Liam must be tired of starting every morning with her screaming in terror. She climbed out of bed and headed toward the bathroom, hoping to avoid further conversation on the matter.

Emma didn't want to talk about it, and she didn't want to hear Liam's gentle reminders that she should schedule an appointment with a counselor. That was not an option. What had happened to her was private, and she wasn't going to open up to a stranger about it. She was embarrassed that she couldn't control her own thoughts.

Liam rolled out of bed and kept his mouth shut. He could tell his wife was in no mood for platitudes and kind words.

Opening the door between the bathroom and bedroom a few minutes later, Emma noticed Liam was no longer there. She assumed he already had the girls up and dressed and had also cooked a gourmet breakfast. It was like being married to Superman. He was practically perfect, and although she loved his generous, giving heart, she was in no mood for it. In her mind, Liam's greatness only magnified her own short-comings.

She grabbed the new maternity jeans and top she'd purchased on Saturday. At least she had some clothes that actually fit over her bulging middle. Trudging downstairs, she found her daughters and her husband eating breakfast. She grabbed a plate and joined them, completely aware that she had a bad attitude.

After walking the girls to the bus, Emma went back inside to grab her purse. Liam was on a conference call with the Chicago office, so he was already in work mode. She waved goodbye and walked next door to Morning Glory.

Her quaint coffee shop was already in full swing when she walked through the door. The cheery blue walls and mismatched furniture always made her smile. The walls boasted a hodgepodge of eclectic decorations, but her favorite part of the shop was the antique pastry display case, which she'd found at a garage sale and restored just before the grand opening.

Jane, the trusty shop manager, was standing behind the

counter recommending the lemon scones to a customer. As she spoke, she started the woman's coffee order, which she knew without being told. She had everything running like clockwork.

"Morning, sweets!" Jane called as she noticed Emma.

Jane's usual blue hair had some new purple streaks as well. Few women could pull off such vibrant hair color, but she managed to do so beautifully. Her tattoos, nose ring, and unique fashion sense suited her bright personality.

"Morning, Jane. I'll be right back. I just want to put my things in my office."

Emma stowed her purse behind her desk, then walked back out front to give Jane a hand with the customer load. She took a few orders and wiped down empty tables, thankful they were so busy.

The next few hours slipped right by, and when she looked, she was startled to see it was two in the afternoon already. She noticed the trash can behind the counter was full, and Jane was still waiting on customers. Gathering the trash bag, she carried it around to the dumpster in the alley behind Morning Glory, opened the lid, and tossed the bag inside.

She was just about to go back inside when she saw a car driving slowly past the alley. It was a fancy black sports car with tinted windows. She had no idea why it had caught her attention, but she continued to stare at it. The sleek vehicle probably cost more than she and Liam earned in an entire year.

The car stopped at the end of the road. It almost seemed as if the driver was watching her. A prickling sensation traveled up the back of her neck, and nervousness lodged in the pit of her stomach. Emma stared at the driver, but making identification was impossible due to the dark tint. Just as quickly as the car had stopped, it took off again.

"That was strange," Emma muttered as she went back inside the building. She made sure to lock the back door behind her.

She told herself it wasn't a cause for concern; she was simply on edge because she was sleep-deprived. She worked in her office for the next hour and a half until it was time to meet the girls, then shut down the computer, gathered her belongings, and told Jane goodbye.

Emma walked next door as the bus pulled up in front. She waved to the bus driver, who motioned the girls safely across the street.

As they headed into the house, Emma glanced behind her and noticed the car she'd seen earlier was parked down the street. She tried not to assume the worst, but she'd become nervous and paranoid since Xavier's attack.

"Pull yourself together, Emma." Ignoring the warning bells in her mind, she went inside for the afternoon ritual of homework and dinner preparation.

As the girls ran up ahead, Emma started singing, "Don't go breaking my heart..."

The girls sang back in unison, "I couldn't if I tried."

It was their own little tradition, something she used to sing to them when they were babies. At that moment, she sang it to convince herself that her life was normal and safe. She sang it to curb the voices inside of her head telling her the black car was a problem. She sang it to console herself with something familiar.

SIX

Tuesday morning flew by quickly at Morning Glory, as most days seemed to do. Emma wasn't feeling very cheerful, though, and she chalked it up to pregnancy hormones. A gray cloud was hanging over her head, and she couldn't quite snap out of her dark mood. She didn't feel like herself.

Her growling stomach reminded her that it was nearly lunchtime, and she needed to eat something. Daisy never let her skip a meal. Emma heard the front door jingle, and Sadie, her lifelong best friend, waltzed through the door. They had a lunch date, and Emma couldn't wait to catch up.

Sadie looked as if she'd stepped out of the pages of *Vogue* magazine in her chic black pantsuit and purple silk scarf. She had the most flawless face of anyone Emma had ever seen in person. Her honey-blonde hair hung loosely to her waist, and her gorgeous cornflower-blue eyes sparkled with goodness and kindness. Perfect white teeth were visible as her plump lips turned up in a smile.

Sadie was a head turner. It was hard not to be jealous of someone so beautiful, but the bond between the two women was so strong that they viewed one another as family, even though they weren't blood relatives. Sadie was just as lovely on the inside as she was on the outside. She had been Emma's rock for years.

"Hey, Emmy." Sadie hugged her friend tightly.

"It's not fair that you look so perfect when I'm awkward and pregnant," Emma whined as she hugged her back.

"Stop it. You are a beautiful and glowing mama."

Sadie placed her hands on Emma's protruding abdomen, leaned down, and whispered, "Hello," to Daisy. Emma giggled, slightly embarrassed, as a few customers looked in their direction. Sadie was so used to attention that she didn't even notice. The women each grabbed a bagel and found an empty booth, Sadie sipping a latte while Emma drank herbal tea.

"How's work?" Emma inquired between bites.

"I'm swamped. We have a huge children's program coming up at the library, and the entire staff is buried with preparations. It's good to be busy. How about you?" Sadie took a drink and munched on her bagel.

"Things are pretty good. I finally bought some new maternity clothes on Saturday. Nothing seems to fit me these days. I was thinking we need a girls' shopping trip soon. It's been ages since we had one."

"That sounds like fun, if you're up to it. I think you should be taking it easy. You look a little pale, even for you, and you have dark circles under your eyes. Are you feeling okay?"

"Yes, Mother, I'm feeling fine. I just haven't been sleeping well lately." Emma looked away from Sadie's concerned gaze. She just knew her friend would push the issue.

"Why aren't you sleeping? Are you still having night-mares, Em?"

Emma couldn't lie to Sadie, so she reluctantly admitted the truth. "Every night. I can't seem to shake them."

"Maybe you should talk to a professional about it," Sadie suggested gently.

"You sound like Liam. I really just want to forget about the whole thing. I mean, it can't last forever, right? Eventually the nightmares will stop." Emma knew she sounded testy, but she wanted to make it clear that the discussion was finished.

Sadie looked concerned but she got the hint, diverting the conversation to the girls and Liam. Emma's tension eased a little. She invited Sadie to come for dinner that evening, and her friend accepted. That was good. The girls would enjoy some time with Sadie, and her lightheartedness might help improve Emma's mood. Sadie had that effect on people.

All too quickly, Sadie's lunch hour ended. She hugged Emma goodbye and returned to the library.

Emma spent the rest of the afternoon in her office. Jane was leaving early, and Emma had to get the girls, so she decided to close the shop early.

After locking the door to Morning Glory, Emma walked home. She tried the front door but found it was locked, so she searched through her purse for the keys. She'd assumed Liam would be home, but he must have had some errands to run.

As she slid the key into the lock, she noticed a small package lying on the porch. She bent down to pick it up and admired the pink baby wrapping paper and expertly tied purple bow. Someone had put a lot of time and expense into decorating the gift. It seemed strange that it had been left on the front porch, and there was no note or card attached.

Emma carried it into the kitchen. With a smile, she tore off the paper, excited to see what was inside. It was Daisy's first baby gift.

As she pulled away the last shred of wrapping paper, she gasped. Her hands trembled as she examined the "gift." It was a handmade stuffed doll whose eyes and mouth were sewn shut. A bloodlike substance was smeared on its hideous face. The handmade dress was embroidered with the name "Emma" across the front.

Panicking, Emma dropped the doll on the counter. Her heart raced and she felt nauseated. Who would leave such a grotesque thing on her porch, disguised as a baby gift? Images of the dead flowers Xavier had left on her porch flashed into her mind. She immediately began to wonder whether this new form of mental torture was tied to him. Perhaps he had escaped from prison and he was stalking her again. She couldn't let that happen.

A shiver trailed down her spine, and she quickly ran to lock the front door. She was terrified that Xavier might somehow find his way into her house again. She tried to convince herself that she and Liam would have been notified in the event of a prison break. Something like that wouldn't go undetected by the authorities. Although she hoped that was true, in her heart she knew Xavier was cunning, evil, and capable of anything. Emma began to pace back and forth, unsure of what to do.

"Don't panic," she consoled herself. "Think about it logically. Xavier is in prison. He's behind bars. He can't hurt you."

She told herself that it was just a prank. After all, it was October. Halloween was right around the corner. A neighborhood kid probably thought it would be funny to scare a pregnant lady. For her own sanity, she had to believe the event wasn't connected to Xavier. It was unlikely that she was being targeted again. Things like that just didn't happen in Beckland.

Glancing at the doll on the counter, her only thought was to get rid of it. If the girls saw it, they would be terrified and disturbed. Then they would all have nightmares. If Liam saw it, he would be irate. She grabbed the evidence and placed it in a black garbage bag. Trying to calm her pounding heart, she walked outside to the trash can and tossed it inside, then wiped the tears that were coursing down her cheeks and went back inside to start dinner.

SEVEN

Liam waved goodbye to the officers at the Beckland police station, grabbed the car keys out of his pocket, and unlocked his Mustang. Turning the key in the ignition, he breathed a sigh of relief to be done with work for the day.

He was collaborating with the Beckland police officers for a local case on which the FBI had become involved. A Beckland businessman who had laundered millions of dollars had finally gotten what was coming to him. It was an open-and-shut case, and Liam was happy to sit in on it. He had seen his share of gruesome, gut-wrenching investigations, so a simple money laundering case was a walk in the park.

He was happy to be heading home to Emma and the girls, and he had a general sense of well-being with his current state of affairs. The women in his life had him wrapped around their fingers, and he wasn't ashamed to admit it. He had a good thing going, and he was grateful every day for his growing family. Other than Emma's lingering nightmares from Xavier's attack, things were pretty close to perfect.

The mere thought of Xavier was enough to set his blood boiling. Liam clenched his jaw and his muscles tensed at the thought of what had happened to Emma. He blamed himself for not getting there sooner the night Xavier broke in. If he had only paid more attention, Xavier wouldn't have been able to get inside of Emma's house. If he had realized sooner that Xavier was Veronica Smith's ex-husband, and that he was searching for her jewel stash, he could have saved Emma from the hell she'd endured at the man's hands.

Every morning when his wife woke in a dead panic from the terror inflicted upon her in her dreams, he grew angrier. It had nearly killed him to see what Xavier did to Emma that night. She was brutally beaten, stripped naked, and tied to a chair. As hard as he tried, Liam couldn't erase that image from his mind.

Xavier was in prison, but he was still torturing Emma, and Liam was helpless to protect her from the dreams. She relived every moment of the attack each night. All he could do was comfort her when she woke trembling, crying, and drenched with sweat.

He tried to convince her to talk to a counselor, but she refused. Liam knew from personal experience that there were times when a professional could help a person work through the intricacies of the mind. A few years before, he'd been working on a horrific case that involved a child. He'd nearly had a breakdown because he couldn't erase the images from his mind. The only thing that got him through it was seeking help.

If only he could convince Emma that talking to a therapist didn't make her weak. He believed pushing the issue with her would make it worse, but he couldn't stand to see his wife so traumatized.

Liam made a promise to himself the night of the attack.

He swore that no one would ever hurt Emma or the girls again. He would protect them with his life, and God help anyone who got in his way.

He took a few deep breaths, tried to push all thoughts of Xavier aside, and pulled into his driveway.

EIGHT

EMMA WAS FINISHING MAKING DINNER WHEN LIAM CAME through the front door. She'd reapplied her makeup so there was no trace of the tears she'd shed over the "gift" left on the front porch. Turmoil bubbled inside of her, but she tried not to let it show.

She didn't want Liam to know anything else was wrong. She'd already made it clear that she couldn't handle the stress in her life, and she wasn't telling him about the doll on the porch, or the black sports car that she thought might be following her.

"Sweetheart, I'm home," Liam called as he shut the front door behind him.

"In the kitchen...," she replied.

She took the pot roast out of the oven and placed it on the stovetop. Liam wrapped his arms around her middle. She breathed in the scent of him, happy he was home. It felt good to have him close after the day she'd had.

Liam grounded her. He reminded her of the things that really mattered in life. She turned toward him and laid her head on his chest. The strong, steady beat of his heart pounded in her ear. She closed her eyes and tried to match her racing heartbeat to his.

"How was your day?" She maintained the connection between their bodies. She didn't want any space between them.

"Uneventful. What happened at Morning Glory?" Liam ran his fingers through Emma's hair.

She swallowed hard and tried to moisten her parched throat. She didn't want him to know anything was wrong. Emma refused to let him know that she feared Xavier was rearing his ugly head once again. She knew it was just her overactive imagination, and she wouldn't give voice to such crazy notions.

"There's nothing new to report." She tried to keep her voice light. "Sadie's coming down for dinner tonight. I hope you don't mind."

"Of course I don't mind. Sadie's family." Liam grabbed a glass from the cupboard, reached into the refrigerator, and poured himself some iced tea.

As if on cue, the front door opened and shut, signaling Sadie's arrival.

"It's me," she called as she entered the kitchen.

"Aunt Sadie's here," Rose yelled loudly. All three girls ran into the room.

"Hello, my munchkins." Sadie laughed as they bombarded her with hugs.

"Why don't you all have a seat at the table? Dinner's ready." Emma grabbed the potholders from the drawer.

"Let me carry that for you." Liam took the pot roast from his wife and placed it on the table.

Everyone took a seat while Emma washed her hands at the kitchen sink. As she did so, her abdomen knotted into a clearly recognizable contraction. She winced in pain and gasped. If she'd been a first-time mom, she probably wouldn't have been able to identify the clenching, cramping pain. Having experienced it three times before, she immediately understood what was happening.

She also knew it was far too early in her pregnancy for contractions. She grabbed the kitchen counter as her body bent involuntarily from the pain. Her sharp intake of breath brought both Liam and Sadie to her side.

"Baby, what's wrong?" Liam's voice was thick with fear and panic.

"Emma, that's the face you make when you're having a contraction." Sadie glanced at the time on the kitchen clock.

Sadie had attended the births of all of Emma's children, so she knew what was happening. Although she'd never been pregnant, she was practically an expert in labor and delivery.

As quickly as it had come, the pain abated. The grip on Emma's abdomen released, and her breathing returned to normal. She wiped her forehead where beads of sweat had pooled. Standing up straight, she read the fear on her daughters' and husband's faces. Even Sadie looked shaken.

"It was a contraction. A pretty big one." Emma's brain fully registered the fact.

"It's too soon for that, right?" Liam looked back and forth between Emma and Sadie.

"Braxton-Hicks can happen early, but I've never had them before," Emma replied.

"Come sit down, Em. You're white as a sheet and sweating." Sadie and Liam led her to the living room, where she rested awkwardly on the sofa.

"Just give me a minute. Sadie, tell the girls I'm okay. They look scared to death," Emma said quietly.

Sadie went into the kitchen and Emma heard her soothing voice talking to the girls. Liam knelt in front of his wife and grasped her hands in his. The fear on his face was obvious, and Emma knew she had to assure him that everything was going to be fine. Although this was her fourth pregnancy experience, it was his first.

"Liam, I'm fine. Sometimes this happens—" Emma gasped as another sharp pain shot through her abdomen.

"That's it. We're going to the hospital, Emma," Liam declared.

She breathed through the pain and waited for it to ease off. Although she didn't want to go to the hospital, she knew he was right. Contractions in the sixth month were nothing to mess with; as much as she wanted to ignore it, she had to take it seriously.

"You're right," she replied quietly. "Go ask Sadie if she'll stay with the girls tonight."

Liam nodded. A few minutes later, he scooped her into his arms and carried her to the front door. The girls stood in a nervous little line. Sadie looked cool and calm. She would hold down the fort.

Emma kissed her daughters and told them she would be home soon. Lily and Dahlia nodded silently, although there were probably a million questions they wanted to ask.

"Does Daisy want to come out now?" Rose's sweet, innocent face looked up at her mother.

"No, sweetie, it's too soon for Daisy to come out. She's just a little bit restless, and I need to be sure everything is okay. I'll be back before you know it." Emma blew kisses as Liam carried her to the SUV and drove quickly to the hospital.

NINE

LIAM CARRIED HER INTO THE EMERGENCY ROOM AT BECKLAND Community Hospital and made a beeline for the registration area. He found a nearby wheelchair and helped her into it, then cleared his throat and attempted to gain the attention of the woman behind the desk.

Emma had warned him that they should be prepared for a long wait, but she'd underestimated Liam's charisma and charm. The admissions nurse blushed when she saw him, and Emma knew exactly how she felt. Liam's presence was a bit intoxicating, and there didn't seem to be a woman who was immune to it.

Oblivious to the woman's reaction, Liam explained the situation. The nurse asked Emma a few questions, and within minutes they were in a room. She'd had no more pains since they'd left home, and she was second-guessing the decision to come to the hospital. Convincing herself it was better safe than sorry, Emma sat on the hospital bed and Liam sat nervously in the chair beside her.

"I'm sure it's nothing." She squeezed his hand and tried to calm his nerves.

"I'll feel better once the doctor tells me that. I just want you and Daisy to be okay." Liam gripped her hand and kissed it tenderly.

"I know," she replied.

Emma had been in emergency rooms before, and she had resigned herself to a long wait. Surprisingly, they heard a knock on the door and the on-call doctor entered the room.

"Hello, my name is Dr. Gladstone." He shook both of their hands. "What seems to be the problem tonight?"

His compassionate eyes did wonders for Emma's nerves. She knew she was in good hands. She explained about the contractions and Dr. Gladstone nodded silently. He made a few notes in her chart, and then he paged a nurse to check her vitals.

As the nurse placed the blood pressure cuff on Emma's arm and the stethoscope on her chest, she sat quietly and prayed everything was fine. For all her assurances to Liam that everything was normal, she'd never experienced this with her other pregnancies. She didn't want him to know, but she was worried.

The nurse wrote the information on the chart and Dr. Gladstone glanced at it. Emma could tell the doctor wasn't pleased with what he saw.

"Have you had problems with your blood pressure before?" Dr. Gladstone asked.

"My blood pressure is always very low. Why? Is there a problem?" She glanced nervously toward Liam.

"Emma, your blood pressure is dangerously high. Your heart rate is abnormally fast. This, coupled with the fact that you've been having some contractions, gives me reason for concern. I'm going to admit you for observation tonight." It was clear Dr. Gladstone was giving an order, not asking for opinions on the matter.

As much as she wanted to object with a million reasons

why she shouldn't be admitted, she knew she needed to listen. Sadie would stay with the girls for as long as she was needed, so she didn't have to worry about her children. It didn't change the fact that she wanted to sleep in her own bed, not in the hospital.

Emma glanced at Liam, who looked far too pale, and nodded in agreement.

"If you haven't had a history of high blood pressure and an accelerated heart rate, it may all be a fluke. But I want to err on the side of caution. Tell me, have you been under unusual amounts of stress lately? Are you eating regularly and getting enough sleep?" Dr. Gladstone asked.

Emma knew she'd epically failed in most of those categories. Her emotions had been out of control, and her lack of sleep wasn't helping matters any. She was worried, stressed out, and exhausted. The only thing she'd been doing correctly was eating. But she couldn't tell the doctor, because it would only worry Liam, so she decided to bend the truth.

"Everything is good. My stress level is normal for a mom of three who owns a business. And I promise you I'm eating regularly. This one never lets me miss a meal." Emma patted her belly and forced a laugh.

Dr. Gladstone instructed her to relax while he began the admissions process. Emma wasn't looking forward to a night in the hospital. She tried to convince Liam to go home and get some sleep, but it was useless. He insisted that he wasn't leaving his wife's side, then called Sadie to let her know what was going on. She was more than happy to hold down the fort at home.

A few minutes later, a nurse wheeled Emma to the elevator and deposited her on the fourth floor, where she'd be spending the unforeseeable future.

After getting settled in her room, Emma admitted that she was exhausted. Her emotions had taken a roller coaster ride, and they finally caught up with her. She scooted to the far edge of the hospital bed, made sure the rail was secure, and patted the space beside her.

Liam knew exactly what she needed, and he wedged his large body next to hers. It was crowded, but neither of them cared. Everything in the world was set right when they were next to each other.

"I love you, Liam," she whispered.

"Love you more. Good night, sweetheart," he replied.

TEN

Emma was rudely awakened at six o'clock the following morning by an unnecessarily perky nurse wanting to take her vitals. She lowered the rail and eased out of bed, trying not to wake Liam in the process. She moved to the chair in the corner so the nurse would have room to work.

Other than the irritation of having her sleep interrupted, her first thought was that she hadn't had any nightmares. It was the first time in four months that she hadn't woken in a cold sweat. It might not seem like a big deal in the grand scheme of things, but even one night of uninterrupted sleep was a victory in her mind. If it could happen one night, then it could happen the next. Maybe her luck was finally changing for the better.

Liam stirred in bed as the nurse finished her morning routine. He had held her all night long, although he clearly didn't have enough room to be comfortable. He opened his eyes, and Emma smiled at him from across the room.

"Morning," she said.

He stretched his large frame and it filled the entire bed. "It's early. Why are we awake?"

"Sorry to disturb you, but I had to check your wife's blood pressure. The good news is that it's lower than last night. The bad news is that it's still higher than the doctor wants it to be. You need to rest more. Go back to bed now," the nurse instructed.

Emma was disappointed that it hadn't returned to normal overnight. She reluctantly climbed back in bed. Liam placed a breakfast order for Emma, then told her he was going home to shower and help Sadie get the girls ready for school. He kissed her goodbye and promised he would be back as soon as possible.

It was still early, so Emma turned off the lights and tried to sleep more. She was determined to get out of there as soon as possible, and resting was the key to getting her blood pressure back into the normal range. She drifted off to sleep and didn't wake again until Liam entered the room almost two hours later. Her breakfast was cold, but she was so hungry that she didn't even care.

Liam had his laptop, which meant he would be working from the hospital room. Emma knew he would be glued to her side for as long as she was there. His devotion was endearing, even if he sometimes went overboard.

A few minutes later, Dr. Gladstone entered the room. He checked over Emma's chart, asked some more questions, and informed her that she would be spending another night in the hospital for observation. It wasn't what she wanted to hear, but she had to listen. She couldn't put Daisy in danger.

When the doctor left the room, she slumped onto the flat hospital pillow. She wanted to go home.

Liam knew she was upset, so he scooted his chair a little closer to the bed and grabbed her hand. "Em, I know that's not the news you wanted, but we have to be safe. You need to rest. That's hard for you to do at home, so being in the hospital is the best thing for you right now."

Liam smiled, and when he gave his wife that lopsided grin, she couldn't help but feel better. "You're right. I'll follow the doctor's orders," she agreed.

Leaning across the railing of the hospital bed, Liam cupped her face and trailed his thumb across her cheek. He gently caressed her lips with his.

"I don't think that's the best way to lower my blood pressure." She giggled between kisses and decided if she had to be confined to a hospital room, there was no one on earth she'd rather be with.

ELEVEN

Thursday dawned sunny, bright, and beautiful. It was everything that a late October morning should be. Emma had received her discharge papers from Dr. Gladstone, and she was on her way home. When they arrived, Liam made her a bed on the couch and told her to stay put. She'd been put on bedrest until the following week, and she wasn't allowed to climb the stairs until then.

She felt horrible for abandoning Jane at Morning Glory, but her trustworthy manager assured her that everything was under control. She knew Jane could handle things, but it made her realize that she needed to hire a second person to cover a few shifts. With a new baby coming, she couldn't expect Jane to run the shop with no help. She was going to want some time off once Daisy arrived, so she made a mental note to put up a Help Wanted sign as soon as possible.

Liam had to go out of town for work for a few days, and he was leaving the following morning. He had tried to get out of it, but he couldn't. Sadie would be staying to help her out while he was gone. He felt guilty, but Emma told him he was being ridiculous. His job was important, and he had to make it a priority. He was an FBI agent, not a nursemaid.

She knew he was worried, but she assured him that she would be fine. She wasn't only saying the words; she really felt optimistic that things had taken a turn for the better. She hadn't had any nightmares while she'd been at the hospital, and she felt amazingly less stressed.

The remainder of her day was spent on the couch, and she was bored out of her mind. She wanted to get up and do something, but Liam watched her like a hawk, so she stayed put. Instead, he ordered lunch from Chen's Chinese Garden, and they watched a movie.

When the girls arrived home from school, he helped them with their homework, finished the laundry, and made dinner. Emma sulked on the couch, frustrated that she couldn't do anything. She felt like she would go out of her mind until she could return to work the following week. Monday seemed like light-years away.

After dinner, she and the girls snuggled on the couch, and her bad mood dissipated. She reminded herself that she should be grateful they were all safe, happy, and healthy.

Once everyone was tucked in for the night, Liam carried Emma upstairs to their room. As she climbed into bed, the melancholy set in. Liam would be gone for three days, and she didn't like it when he was away. Everything felt off-kilter when he was gone.

She placed her head on Liam's chest and listened to the steady beating of his heart. Daisy moved inside of her belly and settled into a comfortable position for the night. Emma felt a sudden intense need to be close to Liam. Lifting her head from his chest, she lowered her lips to his, her pulse quickening.

"I thought you were supposed to be resting." Liam grinned seductively.

"I can rest later. What I need right now is to be close to you. That's the best medicine in the world."

Emma pulled his face toward hers. Their lips met and she lost touch with reality. Nothing mattered in that moment but Liam. Just for a little while, she wanted to exist in a bubble, completely oblivious to the problems of the outside world. Time would pass, morning would arrive, and Liam would have to leave. But that moment was theirs, and she was going to savor every second.

TWELVE

Liam left early the next morning, and Emma's heart sank as she watched him drive away. The minute the Mustang exited the driveway, Sadie entered through the front door. She gave Emma a stern look and told her to resume her position on the living room couch.

"We are going to spend the entire weekend watching chick flicks and eating everything we can get our hands on." Sadie smiled and settled into the comfy chair next to the couch.

"Fine." Emma knew she sounded pouty, but she couldn't help it.

"Cheer up, Emmy. The prison bars will come off the door on Monday. Why can't you just enjoy the break? You never sit still. You do more in an hour than I do in a whole day." Sadie handed Emma the bag of popcorn she'd nearly finished already.

"I want to watch something funny. At least I can laugh if I have to be cooped up in the house all day." Emma crammed popcorn into her mouth while Sadie found the movie.

They spent the next two hours giggling at the antics on television, and Emma forgot about her confinement for a little while. When the movie ended, Sadie prepared lunch and they started another movie. When the credits began scrolling across the screen, the bus rounded the corner and the girls arrived home.

Emma's daughters burst through the front door like shots fired from cannons. The house went from quiet to chaos in a matter of seconds, but it was her favorite time of the day. They greeted their mother with kisses, and she listened to the latest gossip from elementary school.

When the chatter abated, they reluctantly began their homework. Since it was the weekend, the workload was minimal, which made everyone happy. They knew Sadie was spending the whole weekend with them and that meant fun would be had by all. They would do anything to get the festivities started sooner.

Emma was the first to admit that Sadie had her beat in the fun department. The entire weekend was mapped out with exciting entertainment. Later that evening, they would be making nachos and chocolate chip cookies, and then they were all going to watch *The Little Mermaid*. Sadie was taking the girls shopping the following day, and they would order pizza for dinner. Emma suspected the shopping trip was partially to make the girls happy, but also to give her some peace and quiet during the day.

On Sunday, Sadie and the girls would go to church, and then they were getting manicures at On Your Toes Salon. They would bring dinner home to celebrate Liam's homecoming. Emma knew it would be a busy weekend for Sadie and the girls, but she was frustrated that she wouldn't be a part of any of it. All she would be doing was spending time on the couch. It was difficult for her not to wallow in self-pity. Although she knew bedrest was good for Daisy, it didn't make it any easier.

Monday could not arrive soon enough.

THIRTEEN

Xavier Smith

Adjusting the orange jumpsuit on his six-foot muscular frame, Xavier Smith paced back and forth around the perimeter of the prison courtyard as he awaited his allotted time on the bench press. The sun was bright in the sky, and he basked as its warmth radiated on the exposed flesh of his tattooed arms. His cell was dank and depressing, and the only break in the monotony of his daily routine was the time in the yard. After four months in the slammer, he still hadn't acclimated himself to his surroundings.

The thing was he didn't belong there. He was too good for a place like prison. After all, he hadn't killed anyone. Sure, he'd stolen a thing or two, but he hadn't really hurt anyone. He wasn't the same as the cold-blooded killers with whom he was forced to share his days. Technically he had stalked Emma McCoy, or O'Reilly, as she was now known. True, he was forced to rough her up a bit when she didn't cooperate, but that wasn't his fault. If she had listened to him, he wouldn't have had to hurt her. She had brought it all upon herself.

Emma O'Reilly occupied his mind a lot lately, but it wasn't like he had a lot of other things to think about. He certainly wasn't enjoying riveting conversations with the other inmates, so he had a lot of spare time to focus on Emma.

She fascinated him in a way that few women had. She was kind and vulnerable, traits that usually weren't all that attractive to him. In spite of her vulnerability, she was tough as nails on the inside. She had proven that in their brief time together. The woman had surprised him. She wasn't a whimpering baby; she had stood up to him and confronted him, even though he could smell the fear on her.

Perhaps he'd become overly fascinated with her, but that didn't matter. He was drawn to her in the most unexpected ways. It all started when he decided to watch her. He was sure she knew where Jacob and Veronica had stashed the stolen jewels. He'd followed her for months, learning her routine, until he finally broke into her house. What had begun as a simple observation mission had turned into a full-blown obsession.

He thought of Emma all the time. He remembered the way she looked and smelled, the way her flesh had erupted with goose bumps when he ripped her nightgown. He thought of her soft, porcelain skin and the way the blood had trickled down her chest, vibrant and scarlet, when he punched her. She was beautiful. The feel of her velvety skin beneath his fingertips as he traced every inch of her kept him awake at night. He smiled as he visualized the way her body shuddered beneath his touch.

She was stunning and captivating, and she'd taken up permanent residence in his mind. He thought of her, bound to the chair in her kitchen while the dim light from above the stove silhouetted her lovely body. Even though she cried and begged him to stop, he knew she didn't mean it. Deep down, she wanted him as much as he wanted her. It wouldn't have ended so abruptly if Liam O'Reilly hadn't interrupted them.

But Liam had destroyed all the plans he had for Emma. Now all he had were fantasies and thoughts of what might have been. He imagined her every second, played out vivid scenes in his mind. Nothing else mattered to him anymore except Emma.

Xavier wondered if Emma thought about him. They had a connection, and he was sure she felt it that night, but her husband had convinced her that Xavier was evil. He'd probably filled her head with lies about him. More than anything, Xavier wished Emma would walk through the prison doors and tell him she couldn't stop thinking about him.

But so far, she hadn't come. He had only one visitor, who came faithfully every Sunday morning. He should be happy for the companionship she provided, but she wasn't who he wanted, and things always turned ugly between them. Xavier wanted to talk about Emma. He wanted to know about her. His visitor's only job was to bring him information about Emma. He was locked up, so he couldn't find out what he wanted to know without her. The least his visitor could do was tell him what he wanted to know without complaint.

Not only did his companion whine when Xavier talked about Emma, she berated him and told him he was obsessed. She cried and said he cared more for Emma than he did for her. Of course, it was true, but he had to convince her otherwise. He needed the woman to believe he loved her. She had to think they had a future together; otherwise, she would be of no use to him. That was the reason he'd sought her out months before. She was his connection to the outside world, and he needed her. He needed her to watch Emma for him. He needed her to carry out the plan.

So he continued to deny his interest in Emma. He lied to the sniveling, insecure woman and told her his feelings were genuine. He could turn on the charm when it was necessary, and the words he said didn't matter. Xavier knew the truth deep down inside. He and Emma were meant to be together, and once his plan was executed, that would happen.

He looked up as the burly prison guard yelled his name. The guard's voice reverberated throughout the yard, letting Xavier know his visitor had arrived. He was frustrated that his daydreams about Emma had been interrupted yet again. But there would be time to think more about her later. Time was something he had in excess these days.

Squaring his shoulders, Xavier followed the guard into the building, down the lifeless hallways, and into the visitation area. As he walked, he sang "Unchained Melody," a song that always reminded him of Emma. His smooth baritone voice echoed through the prison hallway.

He slumped into the hard chair, looked through the thick glass, and picked up the phone on his side. He focused his charming smile and steel-gray eyes on the desperate woman sitting on the opposite side of the glass.

"Hey, baby," Xavier said with a grin.

FOURTEEN

Emma flipped mindlessly through the channels on the television. It was five o'clock Sunday afternoon, and she was bored out of her mind. The past weekend had been the longest one of her life. She was convinced that her couch would have a permanent imprint of her behind from all the sitting she had done.

The good news was she'd been checked the previous afternoon, and her blood pressure was back in the normal range. She'd been given the green light to return to work the next day, and she couldn't wait.

Sadie and the girls would return soon with lasagna from Vinnie's, and Liam would arrive home within the hour. They'd talked on the phone, but she'd missed him intensely. She never felt like herself when they were apart, and she looked forward to being back together soon.

A key turned in the lock of the front door, and the aroma of oregano and basil wafted into the living room. Sadie and the girls had arrived, and her mouth watered as she anticipated the delicious meal that awaited them.

Vinnie's had amazing lasagna, but the restaurant was also

dear to her heart because it was the location of her first date with Liam. That was the night she knew she loved him. Their deep, unusual connection had been cemented in that restaurant, and it had been her favorite ever since.

"Mama, we missed you today," Rose said as she wriggled onto the couch beside her mother and planted a kiss on her cheek.

"I missed you too, sweetie. The house was way too quiet with you gone. Let me see your nails." Rose displayed her little fingers, and Emma admired the hot pink, sparkly nails.

"They're so pretty! Did you thank Sadie?" Emma twirled Rose's strawberry-blonde curls around her finger.

"Of course I did, Mama. I have manners." Rose rolled her lovely green eyes. Of all the girls, Rose looked the most like her mother.

"You have lovely manners. What was I thinking?" Emma laughed at her daughter.

Dahlia and Lily filed in and greeted Emma, both flaunting their bedazzled nails. Sadie had pulled out all the stops during her weekend stay. She'd spoiled the girls, and they'd loved every minute of it. Going back to the reality of Mom was going to be hard for them.

Sadie was banging around in the kitchen, and the clank of plates and metal sound of silverware told Emma she was setting the table. Sick to death of being relegated to the couch, she went into the kitchen to help.

"Why are you up?" Sadie gave Emma a warning glance.

"I'm free to go back to work in the morning, so I can certainly set the table tonight. I've followed the doctor's orders to the letter all weekend. My behind is numb from all the sitting. I don't want to hear another word." Emma's emerald eyes clashed with Sadie's sapphire ones.

"Fine, be my guest. Set the table." Sadie knew it would do her no good to argue.

As she finished the task, Emma heard Liam's Mustang pull into the driveway. Her heart raced with anticipation as she walked briskly to the front porch to greet her husband. He opened the car door and stepped out, his rugged, muscular body a welcome sight. When he saw Emma on the porch, he flashed a dazzling smile, complete with dimple, and her heart jumped inside of her chest. Liam was home, and all was right with the world once again.

He took the porch steps two at a time and wrapped her into his strong embrace. "I missed you so much, Em."

"Three days felt like an eternity. I hope you don't have another trip planned anytime soon." Emma brought her lips to his.

They came up for air and entered the house hand in hand. They'd barely made it through the entryway before Liam was bombarded by three squealing daughters, who had apparently missed him just as much as their mother.

Once the excitement wore off, they all settled down and made quick work of the lasagna. Tummies were soon filled, and Liam and Sadie cleaned up the kitchen. Emma was instructed to go lie down again, and since she was outnumbered, she knew it was a waste of her time to argue.

It wasn't long before the kitchen was cleaned, the girls were ready for bed, and the following day's lunches were made. Once each chore was checked off the list, Sadie came into the living room and announced that she was heading home.

"As usual, you have gone above and beyond the call of duty." Emma hugged her friend tightly.

"You know I enjoy it. It adds some excitement to my boring life." Sadie giggled, kissed Emma on the top of her head, and left for home.

Lily, Rose, and Dahlia hugged their mother good night, and Liam swung Rose onto his shoulders and herded the other girls upstairs for tuck-ins. A few minutes later, he joined his wife on the couch. It was the first time in days that she wasn't irritated to sit on the sofa. Liam had a way of making everything better.

"I have a surprise for you." His azure eyes sparkled with mischief.

"What is it?"

"If I told you, it wouldn't be a surprise."

"Come on, tell me, Liam."

He reached behind his back, pulled out an envelope, and handed it to her. She opened it excitedly, smiling when she saw it was a gift certificate for On Your Toes Salon.

"Oh my goodness! You got me a prenatal massage, a pedicure, and a manicure? Thank you, Liam." He was such a thoughtful man.

"I knew you would be bummed since you didn't get to go with Sadie and the girls this weekend, so I called and asked her to pick up the gift certificate while she was there. You can go tomorrow, or Tuesday, or whenever you want. All you have to do is call and make the appointment." Liam gave her a lopsided grin, and her heart melted.

"You really are the sweetest man." She leaned toward him and touched her lips to his.

"How much do you like it?" Liam asked mischievously.

"Kind of a lot," she answered with a giggle.

"Maybe you want to come on upstairs and show me." Liam playfully nuzzled her neck, and goose bumps erupted on her skin.

"That sounds like a great idea. And I got the green light to resume normal activity, so…." She wrapped her arms around his neck, and he swept her up and carried her to their room.

FIFTEEN

Emma awoke Monday morning before the alarm went off. Normally she had to drag herself out of bed, but that wasn't the case. After having spent several days practically motionless, she was excited to go back to work. She'd missed Morning Glory, and she couldn't wait to get there. It had been a long time since she'd been so excited for a normal workday.

She had more energy than she'd had in months, partially from days of bedrest, but mostly because of the peaceful sleep she'd enjoyed the past few days. Since her first night in the hospital, she hadn't had a single nightmare. She hoped she could put everything about Xavier behind her. He was officially out of her life.

Liam was still asleep, and she let him stay that way. She prepared breakfast, made a cup of herbal tea, and whipped up some scrambled eggs. When the food was finished, she went from room to room and flipped on the overhead lights to wake her daughters, who were not as enthusiastic about the impending day as their mother. Between grumbles and groans, they finally dragged themselves out of bed and dressed for school. They ate breakfast together, and Liam joined them midway through the meal.

He was working from home, so he would clean up the kitchen. They kissed him goodbye, and Emma and the girls headed out the front door. She herded them onto the bus, then walked the few short steps to Morning Glory.

"Emma! You're back!" Jane greeted her boss enthusiastically as she walked into the coffee shop. "It's so good to see you and your baby bump."

"Well, the bump and I are happy to be back. We've had our fill of couch sitting." Emma hugged Jane and then headed to her office. She checked emails, gave her attention to a few other important tasks, and then went up front to help out.

The morning buzz of the coffee shop bolstered Emma's already great mood. She waited on customers, wiped down tables, and chatted with a few of her regulars. A feeling of happy satisfaction permeated the room.

After the morning rush, she gathered the trash from behind the counter, unlocked the alley door, and walked to the dumpster. She opened the lid and dropped the trash bags inside.

Her hands flew to her mouth to stifle the gasp that erupted. The word *DIE!* was painted in bright red on the underside of the dumpster lid. She was shocked, and she stood there staring at the letters in disbelief. She didn't know what to make of it. The vandalism was on the dumpster dedicated to Morning Glory, so she assumed it was directed at her. Of course, it could have been done by kids who thought vandalism was a joke, but it still made her uneasy.

She needed to tell Liam.

She went back to her office, making sure to secure the alley door behind her, then called Liam and asked him to come next door. Within minutes he was there. He examined the dumpster, checked the alley, and came to the conclusion that there was no evidence to suggest a culprit. There were no cameras in the alley, and he told her it was probably just some kids who were up to no good.

He calmed her nerves and told her not to worry. He said they were installing security cameras immediately, something they should have done before for safety's sake. She felt better just knowing he was on the case. She was also relieved that he didn't believe she was a specific target. She'd been so paranoid since her attack, so she always thought the worst.

Liam tried to convince her to go home for the rest of the afternoon, but she refused. She insisted she would be home at the usual time, and that he shouldn't worry so much. Reluctantly he went home, but she could detect the worry behind his eyes. He was concerned that her blood pressure would skyrocket again.

Emma returned to her desk to finish the paperwork, but she felt the knots of tension in her body. She had to stay calm so her vitals would remain stable; she did not want to be placed on bedrest again. She remembered the gift certificate for the massage, so she called On Your Toes to schedule an appointment.

She dialed the number and spoke with the receptionist, who excitedly said she had an opening in the afternoon. Emma grabbed the appointment, and then she called Liam and told him where she was going. He was more than happy to take charge of the girls for the afternoon. She hung up the phone, eagerly anticipating an afternoon of luxurious relaxation.

After closing Morning Glory a few hours later, she walked the three blocks to On Your Toes. Megan, the perky receptionist, greeted her at the door. She was led into the changing room, given a fluffy robe, and instructed to put it on. Then she was taken to the sitting room and offered herbal tea and homemade cookies. Emma sank into the comfy chair and closed her eyes, listening to the soothing sounds of nature oozing from the speakers as she sipped the tea and waited for her massage.

A few minutes later, Megan returned and led her down the hall to the massage room. It was lit only with candles, and the smell of lavender filled the air. Emma was introduced to her massage therapist, Angela, who asked a few questions before helping her onto the table. She worked her magic on Emma's tired, stressed muscles, and before Emma knew it, she was asleep.

An hour later, Emma woke to Angela's gentle voice telling her the massage was over. Emma was embarrassed that she'd fallen asleep, and even more chagrined when she saw the puddle of drool on the pillowcase. Angela just smiled and said it happened all the time as she helped Emma from the table and led her down the hall to the pedicure area.

She was guided to a chair, introduced to her nail technician, Bethany, and instructed to put her feet into the fragrant, warm, bubbling cauldron of water. By that time, Emma was so relaxed that her body felt like Jell-O. Bethany worked on her feet, massaging, filing, and buffing. Emma closed her eyes and savored the sensation as Bethany continued the pedicure.

Someone sat in the chair next to Emma, and she slowly opened her eyes. To her utter disbelief, she saw that the woman seated next to her was the same woman with whom she'd had the altercation at the mall. She would do anything to avoid another incident with the rude woman, so she turned away and hoped she wouldn't recognize her. Emma lowered her head and allowed her hair to cover her face.

"You have beautiful hair. I would pay big money to get that color. Who does it for you?" The woman's voice was clearly recognizable as the person who had yelled at her.

Emma wasn't sure how to respond. "Thank you. It's

natural," she finally answered. She turned her head slightly toward the woman and offered a weak smile. She anticipated recognition and the subsequent tirade that was sure to ensue.

"Oh, well some women have all the luck, I suppose." The woman made eye contact and smiled widely.

Emma wasn't sure what was happening. Either the woman had amnesia, or she really didn't recognize her. There wasn't even a hint of animosity in her friendly voice. Her blue eyes, the ones that had glared at her accusingly a few weeks ago, were filled with friendliness and cheer.

The transformation was remarkable. Emma remembered her being pretty, but the woman's charming smile elevated her beauty to a whole new level. It was hard to believe that it could be the same woman who'd screamed at her loudly enough to attract a crowd, and who'd plowed into her hard enough to leave a bruise.

"I'm Morgan Turner." The stunning woman leaned across the arm of the chair and extended her perfectly manicured hand.

Emma gave her the benefit of the doubt and returned the handshake. She decided to play along and pretend it was the first time they'd met. She wasn't going to bring up that day at the mall. "I'm Emma O'Reilly. It's nice to meet you. Are you visiting Beckland?"

"I just moved here, and I don't know anyone. I thought I'd treat myself to a pedicure." Morgan smiled widely, revealing perfectly straight, dazzling white teeth.

The two women chatted while the technicians pampered their feet. Emma discovered that Morgan was renting an apartment in Beckland, and that she planned to start looking for work. She confessed that she was starting a new life in a new town, and when Emma commented that Beckland was a little off the beaten path, Morgan said that was precisely why she'd chosen it. Having always lived in large cities, she wanted to try the simple life. By the time Emma's toes were painted a lovely shade of electric blue, Morgan felt like a friend.

As she stood to leave, Emma invited Morgan to visit Morning Glory. She assured her that it was a hub to connect with the locals, and Morgan happily agreed. Emma gave the receptionist her gift certificate, tipped generously for the services, and walked home.

She felt relaxed and happy. Nothing in the world could burst her bubble. Other than the scare at the dumpster that afternoon, it had been a perfect day. She'd even made an unexpected friend.

SIXTEEN

THE SMELL OF ROASTED CHICKEN WAFTED THROUGH THE AIR when Emma walked through the front door. Clearly Liam had prepared dinner. Entering the kitchen, she basked in the sight of her home life on display. Liam and Dahlia were working on spelling, and Lily was setting the table as Rose pirouetted around it, her reddish-blonde curls bouncing delightfully. When she saw her mother, she ran to her and hugged her tightly. Emma squeezed her daughter tenderly.

"Missed you, Mama," Rose said with a toothless grin.

She had recently lost both front teeth, and her adorableness was off the charts. The girls were all growing so quickly, and Emma tried to savor every second.

"I missed you too, sweetie. It smells yummy in here. You guys have been hard at work while I was being pampered." Emma kissed Lily on the cheek before walking around the counter to hug Dahlia. Liam received a lingering kiss, and she thanked him profusely for the afternoon of relaxation he'd facilitated.

"You deserve it. I'm guessing you had a great time?" Liam asked.

"It was amazing. I feel fabulous. I had a pedicure, and I was so relaxed that I fell asleep during the massage. I drooled all over the pillow. I also made a new friend."

She decided it was best to omit the fact that the new friend was the same woman who'd practically assaulted her the previous month. She'd never told Liam, and it seemed pointless to do so now that the women were friends. Emma also thought it might have been a case of mistaken identity. There was no way her sweet new friend was the same woman who'd assaulted her.

"You made a new friend in Beckland? That doesn't happen every day. What do you know about this new friend?" Liam was in full inquisition mode, firing questions in rapid succession.

"Whoa, hold on there, Detective," she said with a smile. "What's with the third degree?"

"It's my job to worry about you. I want good people in your life, and this person is a complete stranger." She could tell he was trying to get his skepticism in check.

"Strangers aren't all bad. Besides, it wasn't long ago that you were the new guy in town. Aren't you glad I gave you a chance?" She grinned mischievously when she saw her arrow hit its intended target.

"Point taken. I'll try not to be so skeptical. Tell me about this wonderful new friend," he conceded.

"Well, her name is Morgan Turner, and she just moved here to start a new life. She wanted to try out a small town. She's renting an apartment and looking for work. She's gorgeous, sweet, and I really like her."

"A new life, huh? Wonder what was wrong with the old one. I guess I'll refrain from the questions I want to ask about that. Maybe you should invite her to dinner sometime so we can all get to know her."

"That's a great idea. Maybe I will." She kissed her suspicious husband on the cheek and pitched in to finish meal preparations.

The family sat down to dinner, and they were all blown away by Liam's culinary skills. His roasted rosemary chicken was delicious. Emma knew he was a much better cook than she was, and she wasn't too proud to admit it. If there was anything her gorgeous husband wasn't good at, she hadn't found it.

After dinner, she convinced him to relax while she cleaned the kitchen and worked on bedtime routines. She and the girls sat on Lily's purple-flowered bedspread, and she read aloud from *Anne of Green Gables* before she tucked each one into bed. She joined Liam downstairs, happy and content with her life.

The couple watched television for a while, then decided to call it a night. She ambled up the stairs and into the bedroom, and Liam followed. They collapsed onto the bed together.

"Do you need a massage?" Liam asked, his dimpled grin making her heart flip-flop inside her chest.

"Well, I'm not going to say no," she answered with a laugh.

His strong hands rubbed her legs, kneading the skin lightly, exactly the way she liked it. When he reached her feet, he stopped. She wiggled her freshly painted electric blue toes at him and laughed.

"Like them?"

"I love them. They look good enough to eat." Liam leaned toward her toes, baring his teeth playfully, and she erupted in giggles.

He drew closer, taunting her with a grin. Her feet were painfully ticklish, and the mere thought of it was enough to send her scrambling awkwardly across the bed. They laughed and played, and she was struck anew at how well they fit together. They always had fun, no matter what they were doing.

"Truce." Emma wiped away the tears that were flowing down her cheeks from laughing so hard.

"Fine. I'll stay away from your feet on one condition. How about you bring the rest of you a little bit closer?"

Emma's heart beat faster as she crossed the bed to where he was sitting. She knelt behind him, massaged his shoulders, and planted soft kisses on his neck. After a few minutes, he turned toward her and kissed her lips gently.

"I love you."

She lost herself in the ocean of his eyes. The world melted away, and nothing mattered but the perfect love that existed within the room.

SEVENTEEN

THE BUZZING OF THE ALARM AT SIX O'CLOCK THE NEXT morning was a rude awakening from peaceful sleep. Emma yawned and stretched her limbs, not wanting to emerge from the cozy cocoon of blankets into the dark, chilly November morning. Yet again, she'd experienced a night of blissful, dreamless sleep. She felt rested and grateful that things were finally getting back to normal. It was past time to bid good riddance to Xavier and his night terrors.

She eased out of bed and pulled her fuzzy robe over her thin pajamas. She heard the furnace kick on . Mornings were getting colder, which she loved. Fall and winter were her favorite times of the year.

Liam wasn't in bed, and she assumed he was downstairs. Emma walked down the hall, turning on lights in her daughters' rooms, telling them it was time to get up for school. As she descended the stairs, she could hear their grumbles and groans, letting her know they weren't exactly eager to greet the morning.

Entering the kitchen, she saw Liam already hard at work on his laptop. He had his favorite coffee mug beside him and a look of intensity on his handsome face. Emma loved observing her husband when he was absorbed in his work. She could almost see the wheels turning in his mind, plotting and puzzling until he finally fit the pieces together that would lead him to solve the case. His forehead was creased and he chewed on the end of his pen, both signs that he was in deep concentration.

Not wanting to derail his train of thought, she quietly went to the cupboard and grabbed a mug for her tea before turning on the kettle. While she waited for the liquid to boil, she set about preparing breakfast for the family. Liam was still hard at work, and she'd learned early on that when he had that look on his face, it was best to leave him alone.

After several minutes, he finally looked up from his work. "Morning, honey."

"Morning. Have you solved it yet?" she asked with a knowing smile.

"Almost. How did you know?"

"I can read you like a book. You have a certain look you get when you're close to cracking a case."

"Hmm, a mind reader. What am I thinking right now?" Liam grinned mischievously.

"Oh, I know exactly what you're thinking, and you know very well that we don't have time for that this morning," she returned.

"I know, I know. You can't blame a guy for trying, though." Liam planted a soft kiss on Emma's lips, an unspoken promise of things to come. "I'm going to get a shower. I'll be back down in a few."

She finished making breakfast, called the girls down to eat, and joined them at the table. She was starving. For the past few months, she would wake up feeling queasy, the thought of food almost more than she could bear. But that had all changed. She was at the stage in pregnancy where she believed she could consume anything she could get her hands on.

She gobbled up her scrambled eggs and toast, finished her tea, cleared the table, and rushed the girls out the front door just in time for the bus. Waving, she went back inside to grab her purse and tell Liam goodbye. He was just coming down the stairs, his hair still wet from his shower.

"I'm going to work now. I hope you catch the bad guys." She grinned at her husband before kissing him.

"The bad guys don't stand a chance." Liam hugged her tightly and told her to take it easy at work. Emma rolled her eyes at his overprotectiveness and closed the front door behind her.

Morning Glory was swarming with customers, so she deposited her purse in her office and grabbed a hot pink apron. As she attempted to tie the strings in the back, she noticed that they kept getting shorter as her abdomen grew larger. At seven and a half months pregnant, she felt as if she were outgrowing everything and everyone around her.

"Just a few more weeks and it'll be back to normal," she consoled herself as she made her way up front to help Jane behind the counter.

She began filling orders, whipping up an espresso, making a fresh pot of coffee, and serving a chai tea latte. She loved being busy, and the buzz of the customers gave her an adrenaline rush. When she'd had the brainstorm to start Morning Glory, she'd had no idea that running a coffee shop would suit her so well. She'd also had no idea how fulfilling it would be. Five years later, she still looked forward to coming to work each day. There weren't too many people who could say that.

She was carrying a white chocolate mocha to the corner table when she looked up and saw Morgan Turner come through the front door. Her new friend was wearing a red off-the-shoulder sweater, gray suede knee-high boots, and skintight jeans that showed off her amazing figure. Her chocolate-brown hair was so shiny that it practically glowed. Every head in the room swiveled in the woman's direction. Emma immediately felt sloppy and underdressed.

Morgan scanned the room until her gaze fell upon Emma. The woman smiled, yet it didn't quite reach her lovely eyes. Emma didn't know her well, but she could tell something was wrong. Morgan looked lost, and Emma's heart constricted with sympathy.

"Hi, Morgan. I'm glad you stopped by. Sit anywhere. Let me finish this order and I'll join you," she greeted.

"All right." Morgan appeared uncomfortable, and she awkwardly chose the table closest to her.

Emma went behind the counter, poured a steaming mug of coffee, and carried it to Morgan. "I assume you like coffee. If not, I can get you some tea instead."

"Coffee is great. Thanks, Emma." Morgan smiled weakly, and upon closer observation, Emma noticed she had been crying.

"How was your first day in Beckland?" Emma smiled. She hoped that with a little coaxing, the other woman would open up about what was bothering her.

"It was okay." Morgan looked as if she wanted to elaborate, but she didn't.

"That doesn't sound very convincing, Morgan," she encouraged.

"Well, let's just say that things didn't really go as planned." Morgan shrugged and took a sip of her coffee.

"How so?"

"I swear I went into every store and shop in town looking for work. Beckland business owners aren't exactly chomping at the bit to hire a stranger without much work experience," Morgan confessed as her eyes filled with tears.

"Well, what work experience do you have?"

"Well… um… none."

"I don't mean to be rude, Morgan, but I'm guessing you're around thirty, right?" Emma hoped she hadn't misjudged her age by too much.

"I just turned thirty last month. Why?"

"Well, how does a thirty-year-old woman get to that point in her life and have no work experience?" Emma wasn't trying to be judgmental, but she was hoping to help in some way. In order to do that, she needed some background on the other woman.

"My parents were very wealthy, and when they passed away, I inherited all of their money. I'm a trust fund baby. I've never worked a day in my life," Morgan revealed with a sigh and a shrug of her lovely shoulders.

"Well, not to be nosy, but why do you need to work now?"

"I didn't budget very well. My lawyer recently informed me that all my money is gone. I have nothing—no home, no place to go, no work experience. I sold my parents' house to pay for back taxes that I never knew I owed. I'm basically out of luck." Morgan shrugged as a single tear coursed down her lovely cheek.

"Morgan, I'm so sorry. Things have hit rock bottom for you, huh?" On impulse, Emma reached across the table and squeezed her hand.

"They really couldn't be any worse, Emma. I don't know what I'm going to do. I had enough to pay two months' rent, but after that, I'm broke and homeless." Morgan's tears flowed freely, and Emma had to do something.

"Don't cry. Things are about to get better for you, Morgan. I have an idea." Emma felt responsible for the woman, and she had to help her.

"What can you possibly do, Emma? Besides, we're practically strangers. Why would you want to help me?" Morgan asked as she wiped her tears.

"Well, I'm a Beckland business owner, and I'm in the market for a new employee. Are you interested?" Emma asked with a smile.

"Of course I'm interested, but I don't know the first thing about working in a coffee shop. Why in the world would you hire me?"

"Because you need a job, and I have a job to offer. My manager is great, and between the two of us, we'll have you turned into a barista in no time."

Emma hoped she sounded more convincing than she felt. Training a thirty-year-old woman who had never worked was going to be rough. Hopefully Jane was up for the task.

Morgan leaped from the booth, hugged Emma tightly, and thanked her profusely. Emma was glad to be able to help. It would be scary to have no money and no one to turn to for help.

"Let's go meet Jane."

Emma took a deep breath and hoped her friend wouldn't hate her too much for the spur-of-the-moment decision.

"Hey, Jane, this is Morgan Turner. She just moved to Beckland, and she's our newest employee," Emma began.

"Employee? I didn't know we were hiring a new employee." Jane raised an eyebrow in surprise.

"I told her you were the best manager in the world, and you would have her squared away in no time." Emma silently pleaded with Jane, hoping she wouldn't flip out in front of Morgan.

"Well, Morgan, it's nice to meet you. I'm assuming you must have a load of experience for Emma to hire you on the spot," Jane said less than enthusiastically.

"Experience?" Morgan asked.

"Yes, experience as a barista. You've been one before, right?" Jane inquired.

"No… um… no, I haven't," Morgan stammered as she looked helplessly at Emma.

"I'll explain the details later, Jane. The important thing is that Morgan needs a job, and I've hired her. I know the two of you will get along just fine." Emma led Morgan to her office to fill out the necessary paperwork, ignoring the daggers Jane shot at her back as they walked away.

When the forms were completed, Emma told Morgan to arrive at six o'clock sharp the next morning, warning her that Jane wouldn't put up with tardiness. Morgan thanked her again and left. Emma took a deep breath and headed back up front, certain Jane was going to have a lot to say about the situation.

"Look, I know you're the boss and all, but what the heck?" Jane implored as soon as she saw Emma.

"I know, I know. I'm sorry I didn't discuss it with you. She has no money and no job, Jane. What was I supposed to do? No one else in town is going to hire her, and you know it." Emma shrugged desperately, hoping to convince her.

"Fine, Emma. I'll do my best with her, but you know how I feel about pretty little rich girls, and it's obvious to me that's what she is. All I can say is that she'd better be ready to work. If not, you're going to have to fire the pampered princess." Jane turned on her heel and walked away.

Emma and Jane finished out the afternoon side by side. Emma knew Jane wasn't happy with her decision, but she kept quiet about it. When the school bus rounded the corner at three thirty, she saw Liam walk the girls inside. He would get them started on homework, and hopefully make dinner as well. Emma was staying until five o'clock to help Jane close up shop. It was the least she could do considering what she was asking of her.

When the last customer left for the day, Emma locked the front door, turned over the Closed sign, and wiped down all the tables. Both women restocked supplies for the following morning, and once the prep work was completed, they decided to call it a day.

"Thank you," Emma said as she pulled Jane into a tight hug.

"For what?"

"For being an amazing friend and manager. I know Morgan might be a little difficult, but if anyone can teach her, it's you."

"Mmm-hmm. All I'm saying is the first time she cries because she broke a nail, I cannot be held responsible for my actions." Jane scowled.

EIGHTEEN

At eight thirty the next morning, Emma headed to Morning Glory. Morgan and Jane had been together for two and a half hours, and she prayed they hadn't killed one another.

Glancing through the front window, she noticed Jane was simultaneously juggling approximately five chores, while Morgan stood behind the counter examining her nails and looking bored. Emma rolled her eyes. There was no doubt that Jane was ready to blow her top, and it was her job to run interference.

"Morning, Jane." Emma forced cheerfulness into her voice.

Jane glared at her boss and Emma mouthed, "I'm sorry," as she ran to her office to grab an apron.

Clearly things were not going well. Emma had no idea what had taken place, but from Jane's angry eyes and clenched jaw, she was guessing Morgan hadn't been a great student. It was going to be a long day.

"How are things going? Are you catching on?" Emma asked Morgan as she walked behind the counter.

"I don't think so. I'm really not good at this whole work thing. According to Jane, I don't know how to do anything at all." An angry look passed over Morgan's beautiful face.

Emma noticed that Morgan looked quite menacing, but she reminded herself that it was because of the stressful day she was having. There was definite friction between Morgan and Jane. Their personalities weren't exactly compatible, and Emma had basically thrown them into the ring to fight it out.

"Well, I'm here to help now. I'm sure you'll figure it all out in no time. First days are always hard." Emma patted Morgan's back and led her behind the counter, where she attempted to demonstrate how to make a pot of coffee.

Unfortunately, it didn't take long for Emma to realize that Jane was correct. She didn't know how to do anything. She dumped the coffee grounds all over the floor, and managed to spill half of the water when she completely missed the coffee pot reservoir. Emma could not believe that a grown woman didn't know how to make coffee, and if she couldn't even manage that simple task, things were not going to be easy.

Emma knew with certainty that she'd made a huge mistake in hiring the woman, but there was little she could do about it. She wasn't about to fire Morgan, knowing she had no money. She would simply have to work with her until she learned. Emma had three children, and she was raising them to be competent human beings. Surely she could do the same with Morgan.

"Oops. Sorry," Morgan said as she stared at the coffee grounds and water puddled on the floor below them.

Rather than move to clean up her mess, she just stared at Emma, who instinctively grabbed the broom, dustpan, and a towel to wipe up the water. Across the room, Jane stopped what she was doing and watched what was happening. Anger danced in her gray eyes as she glared at Morgan.

"Emma, stop. Morgan made the mess, and she can clean it up. You're seven and a half months pregnant. You have no business crawling around on the floor to clean up after a woman who is capable of doing it herself."

Jane marched behind the counter, grabbed the broom and towel from Emma's hands, and placed them into Morgan's. The woman just stared at them as if she had no idea what to do. Without another word, Jane took Emma's arm and led her into the office.

"Jane—" Emma began.

"Stop, Emma. Just stop. I have spent the last two and a half hours with that woman, and let me tell you, Rose is more of a grown-up than she is. She doesn't want to work. She doesn't want to do anything. Every time I tried to explain something, her eyes glazed over like I was speaking a foreign language. She has got to go!" Jane paced the room, running her hands through her blue hair in desperation.

"I know you're frustrated with her, but I just can't turn her away with nothing. I feel sorry for her, Jane. She has no one." Emma tried to explain that she felt somehow responsible for the other woman.

"Emma, I love you, and I think you are the kindest woman I have ever known. But kindness has to have some limits. She's worthless!"

"Let's just give her a few more days." Emma pleaded for Jane's understanding.

"I suppose so. I mean, you're the boss after all," Jane relented.

The women walked back up front and noticed Morgan had figured out how to use the broom. She had cleaned up the coffee grounds and was working on the spilled water. Jane and Emma exchanged a glance and went back to work.

As Emma refilled a customer's coffee cup, she saw it was

almost noon. Sadie would be arriving for lunch, and Emma was excited to see her.

As if on cue, her best friend sauntered through the front door, looking like perfection in her red dress and black knee-high boots. She came over, hugged Emma, and grabbed a blueberry muffin and coffee from behind the counter, then stopped dead in her tracks as she noticed Morgan. The two beautiful women eyed one another suspiciously. Sadie locked her sapphire blue eyes onto Morgan's icy blue ones. Neither spoke.

"Sadie, this is Morgan Turner. She's new in town, and she's also my new employee. Morgan, this is Sadie Ross, my best friend." Emma hoped the introduction would break the awkward silence.

"Hello, Morgan." None of Sadie's usual warmth came through in her voice.

"Nice to meet you, Sadie," Morgan replied, although her face didn't reflect her words.

It seemed the women had taken an immediate dislike to one another, although Emma had no idea why. Attempting to end the tense moment, Emma linked her arm through Sadie's and led her to their favorite table. Morgan watched them walk away with a look of jealousy on her face.

"What's up with her?" Sadie jumped in as soon as they sat down.

"What do you mean?" Emma answered.

"Why on earth did you hire her, Emma? She's a complete stranger! Not to mention the fact that there is something off about her. I don't like her." Sadie glanced Morgan's way.

"How could you possibly know that? You just met her twenty seconds ago."

"I'm an amazing judge of character, and my intuition never fails me. You know that. I can't believe you hired her. Is she a professional barista or something? Were her skills so amazing that you hired her on the spot?" Sadie was in rare form.

"No, actually she has no experience whatsoever, if you must know." Emma felt like she was being attacked, and she didn't like it one bit.

"When you hired Jane, you made her go through approximately six interviews and five background checks. Morgan saunters into town and you hire her on the spot? That's not like you."

"I know, but I felt bad for her, Sadie. She's fallen on hard times, and I want to help her." Emma had no idea why Morgan's story had gripped her so tightly, but it had.

"You're always looking out for everyone. That's one of the things I love most about you. But people take advantage of that." Sadie took a bite of her muffin and contemplated her next words. "All right, I'll leave you alone about her. But be careful. I don't trust her."

"Once you get to know her, you'll change your mind." Emma was certain that Sadie and Morgan would be great friends once they got better acquainted.

The women chatted for the remainder of Sadie's lunch break, and then she headed back to the library. Morgan had refilled the sugar containers on the tables, and Emma was relieved that she hadn't made a mess of anything else. That was progress for sure.

"Sadie is really beautiful," Morgan said as she joined Emma behind the counter.

"She is." Emma smiled.

"How long have you been friends?"

"Basically since birth. Our moms were friends, and we grew up together. She's like a sister to me."

"Hmm… well, I don't think she liked me very much. She's probably just threatened because you have a new friend." Morgan put her arm around Emma's shoulders.

"I'm sure that's not the case."

"Women don't usually like me. They see me and think I'm beautiful, and they're jealous of me. Jane doesn't like me either. You're not like the rest of them, Emma. You're truly a kind person." Morgan kissed Emma on the cheek. "I'm going to empty the trash now. Jane showed me how earlier."

Emma watched Morgan walk to the trash can, grab the bag out of it, and head out the back door to the dumpster.

She smiled to herself. Maybe things were going to work out after all.

NINETEEN

Xavier Smith

Xavier squirmed in the uncomfortable chair in the cold, dank meeting room. He thought the least they could do was provide a decent chair to sit in for his only contact with the outside world. He hated Sunday, visitors' day, more than any day of the week.

He looked at the faces of his fellow prisoners, eagerly anticipating visits from their friends and families. Xavier dreaded the time alone with his one and only visitor. It was always the same. She waltzed in, seemingly anxious to see him, poured on the affection, pretended to care, and then became cold and unfeeling the minute he asked the simplest questions about Emma. She said she was in love with him, but she didn't know the first thing about it.

Women were all the same, only interested in themselves. He was convinced that all females were coldhearted snakes, only caring about what they could take from him. Xavier had known more than his share of women, and they were all alike.

His ex-wife, Veronica, had been like that. He gave her his heart, and she stomped on it, ditching him for Jacob McCoy the first chance she got. Well, good riddance to her. Pretty little Veronica got what she had coming to her in that plane crash. He couldn't have planned it better if he tried, and he had definitely plotted his revenge against Veronica. Ironically, fate had taken the responsibility out of his hands, and it had all worked out just fine, in his opinion.

Xavier only knew one woman who didn't fit the description of the ruthless viper, and that was Emma. She was perfect in every way. Her beauty and gentleness called to him, capturing him like no one else had. She was kindness and light. They were meant to be together. He had been told that he was fundamentally broken, and that might be true, but Emma would know how to fix him. He had thought about nothing else for months, and he'd finally come up with a way to make it happen.

Of course, the situation being what it was, he was going to need some help. There was only so much he could do from behind bars. Luckily, throughout his years of not-so-honest living, he had acquired associates who were more than happy to help him. The only thing standing between him and the woman he wanted was Liam O'Reilly.

That uptight Fed may have brainwashed Emma into thinking she loved him, but Xavier knew better. All he needed was some time alone with her, to get her away from Liam long enough to convince her. He had to separate them. Plans were already underway, and soon the path would be clear. Liam wouldn't know what hit him.

He needed a distraction, a way to take the attention off himself when he broke out of prison. The breakout would be the easy part. But before that could happen, he needed to orchestrate the rest of his agenda. That's where his associate came into play. His plan was sheer perfection, with every detail carefully calculated. It was going to be perfect.

Xavier was pulled away from his thoughts when his visitor arrived. This particular part of the plan was the most crucial. In order to facilitate the scheme, she must be willing to assist him. Not that it would be an issue. He knew just what to do. Xavier, being an intensely attractive man, could turn on the charm and use it to get what he wanted. It was child's play. He loved a good game, and it was almost too easy.

As she approached, he greeted her with his hundred-watt smile. Her cheeks turned pink as she bit her lip, and he knew everything would be just fine. She was putty in his hands. Her skills would be extremely useful to him. Before long, Liam and Emma would be ripped apart. Their days were numbered. Like pawns in a game of chess, he would move them all at his will.

TWENTY

Emma finished wiping tables at Morning Glory. She was eager to get home and start dinner. Liam had agreed to invite Morgan over for dinner, and she was excited for the two of them to meet. Morgan had been working at Morning Glory for two weeks, and Emma believed she was getting better every day, although Jane and Sadie didn't share her opinion.

Emma had to admit that Morgan was a bit spoiled, and she wasn't exactly eager to work, but she believed the woman was trying, although Sadie and Jane disagreed. Emma hoped Liam would like her new friend as much as she did.

Morgan was already gone for the day, and Emma let Jane go early as well. It had been a slow day at Morning Glory, and they both deserved a break. She could handle closing up the shop on her own.

After finishing the next day's preparations, she locked up and went home.

As Emma stepped through the front door of her cozy house, she was bombarded by her daughters. They wanted her attention, and she was happy to give it to them. They seated themselves in the kitchen and everyone began talking at once, anxious to fill her in on the day's events. Emma listened patiently to each girl, commenting here and there as they chitchatted. Liam had already started dinner, so she only needed to finish it.

She enjoyed all of the time Liam had been able to spend at home the last few weeks. It wasn't common in his line of work, and she had a sneaking suspicion that he had requested some form of light duty since she was having pregnancy complications. She hadn't asked, but she knew something was up because he was always close to home. The lasagna he'd made smelled wonderful. She'd lucked out to get a loving, hardworking, handsome husband who was equally as mesmerizing in the kitchen. She gave him a quick kiss and sent him upstairs to get ready for their guest.

While she set the table and prepared some iced tea, she helped the girls with their homework. A glance at the clock told her Morgan would be arriving any minute. Emma hustled the girls out of the kitchen, instructing them to take their backpacks to their bedrooms and wash up for dinner.

As Liam rejoined her in the kitchen, Emma smiled. He had changed into his faded jeans and blue button-down dress shirt, which perfectly accentuated his eyes. His hair was freshly washed and curling over his ears, just the way she liked it. The smell of soap and cologne intermingled, creating an inviting scent. The man certainly knew how to make an entrance.

"You smell yummy and look even better," she said as she pulled him close.

"Well, I didn't want to embarrass you in front of your new friend," he replied with a roll of his eyes.

"I don't think you could ever embarrass anyone. Quite the contrary, in fact." She grinned back at him.

Emma carried iced tea to the table while Liam pulled the lasagna out of the oven. A quick glance around the kitchen told her they were ready for Morgan's arrival. For some reason, she felt a bit nervous. She really wanted Liam's approval of Morgan, mostly because every other important person in her life had disliked the woman immediately.

The doorbell chimed and Emma made her way to the front door. Morgan greeted her with a dazzling smile, and Emma was a bit taken aback by her friend's appearance. It was clear that the other woman was out to make a statement. Emma thought that perhaps she'd been unclear about the dinner plans, because Morgan looked more ready to walk the red carpet than to have dinner in the kitchen.

Morgan had on a little black dress, with the emphasis on little. It was strapless, and showed off her flawless skin and ample chest. Morgan's legs were a mile long, and the dress covered very little of them. Her beautiful hair was perfectly swept into a French twist, and delicate drop-pearl earrings adorned her ears. To top it all off, she had on red stilettos. Her beauty nearly took Emma's breath away, and she did nothing but stare for a full minute.

Finally regaining her senses, Emma invited her inside. Morgan always looked good, but that night she was at an entirely different level. The weary mother of three had never felt more awkward or unattractive in her life than she did at that moment. In stark contrast to her lovely dinner guest, Emma was still wearing the clothes she'd worked in all day. She hadn't even glanced at her hair or makeup since that morning. She struggled to find the correct words.

"Wow... Morgan, you look... beautiful." Emma tried to keep herself from gawking at her friend.

"Thank you. I know I'm a little fancy, but I have so few occasions to play dress-up these days." Morgan giggled.

"Well, come on in and meet my family." Emma led her into the kitchen.

Liam was washing his hands at the kitchen sink, and the

girls were already seated at the table, chatting animatedly. All conversation stopped when the women entered the room.

"Morgan, this is Lily, Dahlia, and Rose." She pointed to each girl.

"Man, you sure are pretty. You look just like a princess!" Rose exclaimed while she continued to stare.

"Thank you." Morgan looked uncomfortable.

Lily and Dahlia stared wide-eyed at the stranger but said nothing. So far, Morgan was making quite an impression.

"Morgan, this is my husband, Liam. Liam, this is Morgan." Emma watched her husband closely, expecting him to be as enamored as her daughters.

"It's so nice to finally meet you, Liam. Emma didn't tell me you were so handsome." Morgan sauntered over to Liam and extended her hand, batting her eyelashes almost shamefully. "Emma, it's no wonder you keep him so well hidden. I'll bet women are constantly throwing themselves at him."

A sharp twinge of jealousy tried to push its way to the surface, but Emma did her best to ignore it. As she looked at her friend standing beside her husband, the first thought that came to mind was that they looked like a couple—a painfully exquisite, perfect couple. Emma suddenly felt embarrassingly inadequate as she watched Morgan flirt shamelessly with Liam.

But rather than fall under Morgan's spell, Emma noticed that Liam looked uncomfortable. He crossed the room and stood next to Emma as he pulled her close.

"Emma doesn't keep me hidden at all. I've been busy with a case I'm working on. I've heard a lot about you, Morgan. It's good to finally meet you." Liam's words sounded half-hearted.

Emma knew immediately that Liam wasn't impressed with her friend. At that particular moment, she wasn't impressed with the woman either. She couldn't believe

Morgan showed up dressed like that. She was astonished that Morgan had the nerve to flirt with her husband right in front of her. She didn't know what to do. She considered asking Morgan to leave, but she would never do something that rude. Instead, she showed Morgan to the table and tried to regain her composure.

Emma told herself that she needed to get a handle on her jealousy. It was probably just her pregnancy hormones going crazy. She must be imagining something that wasn't there. Morgan was her friend. She was beautiful, and she liked to dress up when she had an opportunity. There was nothing wrong with any of that. She was used to having men fall all over her, and flirting was second nature. Emma berated herself for being an ungracious hostess. She needed to remember her manners.

She took a breath and joined everyone at the table. Morgan was seated to Emma's right, and Liam sat at the head of the table on her left. She tried her best to think of conversation starters, but nothing came. Instead, Lily took charge of the conversation.

"Are you married?" Emma's oldest daughter blurted as she stared at Morgan.

"No, I'm not." Morgan said tersely.

She didn't elaborate, and she looked annoyed at having to answer Lily's question. Emma took note of the fact that the woman's people skills were sorely underdeveloped, and she didn't appear to have much patience with children.

"Where are you from?" Dahlia's question came across in a much kinder way. The little girl twirled her blonde curls and looked apprehensively at their guest.

"Oh, I'm from here and there." Morgan's answer was vague, and once again, she didn't elaborate.

"What brought you to Beckland?" Liam asked then.

The transformation in Morgan was obvious. She angled

her perfect body toward him and smiled brightly, giving him her full attention.

"Oh, I wanted a change. The thought of a small town was appealing to me. Folks here haven't been exactly delightful, but Emma was so kind to give me a job. Isn't she just the sweetest?" Her words sounded condescending and patronizing.

"Yes, Emma is definitely sweet. It's one of the things I love the most about her." Liam glanced at his wife, and she could tell that things weren't going well.

They continued to eat in silence, and Emma kept trying to think of things to talk about. For some reason, her mind was blank. Liam could generally make conversation with anyone, but he sat quietly eating his lasagna. Morgan picked at her food, and Emma realized that she hadn't even asked if she liked lasagna.

"Is your food okay, Morgan? You haven't eaten very much. If you don't like it, I can make you something else."

"Oh, I'm sure it's just fine, Emma. I'll let you in on a little secret. I don't eat carbs. I have to watch my figure, you know. If I ate like this every day, I wouldn't fit into any of my clothes." Morgan laughed and rolled her eyes. It made Emma feel embarrassed and ridiculous.

She glanced at her own plate, which was basically empty. Emma generally ate what she wanted and didn't give it a second thought. Clearly that's why she didn't look like Morgan.

"Well, I'm guessing that means you won't be having any of the chocolate cake I made for dessert," Emma joked, trying to make light of the awkward situation.

"Cake? You're kidding, right? I can't even remember the last time I ate cake. Single ladies like me have to watch ourselves if we want to snag a man. We don't have the luxury of letting ourselves go." Morgan winked, and Emma had no idea how to respond.

"Well I, for one, would love some cake. Would you girls like some?" Liam spoke loudly, interrupting the uncomfortable tension in the room.

All three girls nodded vigorously, and Liam pushed his chair away from the table and went to the kitchen. Emma stood and began clearing the table, trying to find something to do with her hands. As much as she had been looking forward to a slice of that cake, she certainly wasn't going to eat a piece after that statement. Morgan would be horrified if she gorged herself on dessert after eating all her dinner.

They attempted to make awkward small talk for another half hour. The girls tried again to engage Morgan in conversation, to no avail. She did chat with Liam, however, continuing to ask about work while she gave him her undivided attention. Liam was polite, but he didn't do much more than answer the questions she asked.

"Well, I need to get going. I'm sure you need to do your mommy thing, Emma, and I don't want to get in your way. The whole domestic world sounds like a lot of work to me. It's probably fine for you, though. Some women were just cut out for that, I suppose." Morgan rose from the table.

"It was nice to meet you, Morgan." Dahlia could always be counted upon for politeness and good manners.

Morgan flipped a dismissive wave at the girls and sauntered toward the front door. Liam and Emma followed.

"It was wonderful to finally meet you, Liam. Don't be a stranger. I hope to see you again really soon." Morgan placed her perfectly manicured hand on his arm.

Liam took a decisive step backward and put his arm around his wife. Emma gave Morgan a weak smile as she headed outside and got into her car.

That hadn't gone exactly as planned.

Emma was shocked and embarrassed by Morgan's behavior, and she wondered if maybe she had missed something that everyone around her seemed to see.

The girls finished their cake, and Emma told them to get into their pajamas and brush their teeth. She and Liam cleaned the kitchen, working side by side without saying anything.

Emma wasn't sure how to put her thoughts into words. She'd gone on and on for weeks about how much she liked Morgan, and then the woman had flounced into her home, flirted with her husband, and was rude to her daughters. Then again, maybe she was just being ultra-sensitive.

"What did you think of Morgan?" Emma asked her husband later that night as she undressed for bed.

"Well, she was definitely dressed up." Liam laughed uncomfortably.

"Yeah, she was a little overdressed for family dinner, huh? She's really pretty, though, isn't she?" Emma hoped her insecurity couldn't be heard in her voice.

"I suppose some people might think that. I don't really notice anyone but you, though. Anyway, I prefer strawberry blondes." Liam pulled his wife onto the bed next to him.

"Did you like her? She's nice, right?" Emma snuggled close to her husband.

"Nice? I don't know if that's a word I'd use to describe her, Em. There's something about her that didn't sit right with me. She seemed shallow and self-centered. I don't know what you two could possibly have in common. She's not your usual type of friend."

"You sound like Sadie and Jane," Emma said defensively.

"Sadie and Jane are good friends."

"I know Morgan's a little different, but everyone just needs to give her a chance. She's got some good qualities." Emma wasn't certain if she believed her own argument.

"Just be careful with her, Em. You're kind and generous and always want to believe people are good. Sometimes they're just not. I don't want to see you get hurt." Liam hugged her tightly.

"I'll be careful. Besides, what could she possibly do to hurt me?" Emma snuggled under the blankets next to Liam.

She was more convinced than ever that Morgan was just misunderstood. Maybe her friend was insecure and tried too hard to make people like her. She must have some goodness inside, and Emma was determined to find it.

At that moment, though, she had one pressing thought on her mind.

"Liam," she whispered.

"Hmm?" he answered, almost asleep.

"I really want a piece of chocolate cake."

Emma got out of bed, snuck down to the kitchen, and loaded up on carbs, not giving her figure a second thought.

TWENTY-ONE

AFTER MEETING THE GIRLS AT THE BUS STOP THE NEXT afternoon, Emma drove across town to Beckland Ballet Academy. Lily had ballet class, and they were running late. Emma tried to ignore the angry looks she received from her oldest daughter; to her rigid, structured daughter, unless she arrived at the studio at least fifteen minutes early, she was late.

"Lil, we're going to get there on time. Don't be so stressed out. You'll still have time to change into your leotard and get your bun fixed." Emma tried to smooth over her daughter's anxiety.

"You know Miss Kristin gets really upset if we go into class even a minute late." Lily scowled from the back seat.

"For the millionth time, Lily, you aren't going to be late," Emma argued, but she knew it was futile.

"Well, I'm not going to be early, and that's the same thing as being late."

Lily twisted her long wavy blonde hair up into a perfect ballet bun. She had done it so many times over the years that she could practically do it with her eyes closed.

"We're here. I'll let you out at the door and then find a parking spot." Emma pulled up in front of the dance studio.

Lily jumped out of the car and ran inside. Emma drove around until she found an empty spot. Rose and Dahlia were home with Liam, so she had an entire hour and a half to herself. Instead of going into the studio, she decided to take a walk around the neighborhood.

It was a beautiful fall day, and it might be one of the last decent ones of the year. The temperatures were dropping steadily as they headed into the middle of November. Snow wouldn't be too far away.

Emma strolled leisurely around the neighborhood, stopping to window-shop and say hello to a few familiar folks. The trees were steadily losing their leaves, but the colors that remained were like a beautiful painting.

Emma walked a while longer and soon found herself back at the studio. Feeling refreshed and invigorated, she went inside and found a seat in the observation area, where she watched with pride as Lily finished her class.

Her oldest daughter had started taking ballet at two years old, and she'd never looked back. It was her passion, and she was extremely driven and dedicated. There weren't too many girls her age willing to give up as much free time as Lily did for her classes and rehearsals. Emma was extremely proud, and she smiled as Lily leaped and jumped gracefully across the floor. Maybe she was biased, but Emma believed Lily was a gifted dancer who had the skill to make all her dreams come true.

Class ended and Emma waited while Lily chatted with her friends and changed her clothes. Ten minutes later, Lily finally emerged from the dressing room. As they headed to the car, Lily talked about her class and the technique on which they'd focused.

They reached the car and Emma unlocked the doors. Lily

got into the back seat, and Emma walked around to the driver side. She dropped her keys and awkwardly bent down to pick them up. As she did, she did a double take. All four of the tires on her vehicle were flat.

How does a car get four flat tires at once? A warning bell went off in her brain as she realized it was no accident. It was a malicious trick, and Emma knew immediately that it was absolutely done on purpose.

"What's wrong, Mama?" Lily opened the car door, and Emma saw the worry lines creasing her daughter's brow.

"Well, our tires are flat. Just stay put. I'm going to call Daddy." Emma grabbed her cell phone and dialed Liam's number.

It rang several times before going to voice mail. She hung up and tried again, dismayed that there was still no answer. Emma knew he was probably fixing dinner and helping the girls with homework. He wasn't paying attention to his calls.

She scrolled to Sadie's number and dialed. Ring after ring with no response sent Emma's anxiety level up another notch. Sadie was probably still at work. Emma could call Jane, but she was covering the shift at Morning Glory.

She was about to try Liam again when headlights approached and a shiny black sports car pulled up behind her vehicle. The driver of the car slowed, rolling down the darkly tinted window. Emma breathed a sigh of relief when she saw it was Morgan.

"Hey, Emma." She smiled brightly. "What are you up to?"

"Morgan, thank goodness you're here. My tires are flat. Can you believe that? Would you be able to give Lily and me a ride home?"

"Sure. I can't believe that happened to you, Emma! What horrible luck. Climb on in and I'll have you home in no time." Morgan smiled welcomingly.

Lily and Emma jumped into the fancy car and buckled

up. She couldn't imagine owning a car that nice, and she didn't know anyone else who could afford such a luxury. Emma was so grateful for the rescue that she babbled on and on.

"You are a lifesaver, Morgan. I was just about to panic when you pulled up. Liam and Sadie didn't answer, and I wasn't sure who to try next. It was our lucky night, I guess."

"I'm happy I showed up when you needed me. I was just headed home after my workout, so you'll have to excuse the mess I'm in." Morgan batted her eyelashes.

Emma looked at the other woman and couldn't believe she considered herself a "mess." Morgan was dressed in designer work-out gear, her hair was in a cute, perfect ponytail, and instead of looking like a sweaty mess, she resembled a model in a fitness magazine, complete with the perfect body.

"You have no idea what a mess looks like until you've seen me work out." Emma giggled as she visualized the torn sweat pants and holey T-shirt she wore when riding the exercise bike that was currently being used as a clothing rack in her bedroom.

Morgan pulled up in front of the house. Emma thanked her again for the rescue as she helped Lily out of the back seat.

"Really, Emma, it was my pleasure. You've done so much for me since I came to town. You know, you're really the only friend I have." Morgan waved as she pulled away.

Lily and Emma went inside and found Liam and the girls in the kitchen.

"Hey, honey. I didn't hear you pull into the driveway." Liam kissed his wife as he helped her out of her coat.

"That's because I didn't. Girls, can you please run upstairs and wash up for dinner? I want to talk to Daddy for a minute." Emma smiled at her daughters as they did what she'd asked. She wanted to tell Liam what was going on without scaring them.

"Em, what's wrong?" Worry was written all over Liam's handsome face.

Emma had been holding the words inside since she'd seen the tires, and they all came rushing out at once. "When Lily and I came out of ballet tonight, all four tires on the SUV were flattened. This is obviously not a coincidence. Four tires don't flatten at the same time, unless someone purposely does it. I didn't want to worry Lily, but I was terrified. Who would do this?"

"How did you get home? Why didn't you call me?" Liam was worried, and Emma knew the wheels were already turning inside his head.

"I did call you. And I called Sadie. Neither of you answered your phones." Emma smiled so he would know she wasn't blaming him.

Liam walked over to the counter and grabbed his phone, frowning as he looked at the display. She knew it would say there were two missed calls from her, and she also knew her husband was berating himself for not being there to rescue her when she called him.

"Honey, I'm so sorry. I silenced the phone earlier when I was working, and I guess I forgot to turn it back on. The girls and I were doing homework and making dinner, and I didn't even think to check—"

"It's okay. I knew that was what you were doing. It's not a big deal." The last thing she wanted was for Liam to beat himself up over it.

"It is a big deal. You called and I didn't answer. You needed me and I didn't help you."

"Liam, it all worked out. Morgan happened to be driving by the studio on her way home and saw us. She drove Lily and me home." Morgan had really saved the day.

"That was nice of her. I'm glad she was there. That was lucky." Liam's forehead was creased with worry.

"See, she's not so bad after all, is she?" Emma was happy that her new friend had gained some points with her husband.

"Maybe she's not. I'll have to thank her for helping you next time I see her," Liam conceded.

Emma gently reminded him about the real problem at hand. "We do have to find a way to get the car home. We can't just leave it there."

"You're right. I'll call a tow truck. I need to take a look at those tires and see if I can figure out who did this and why. I don't like it, Emma. It was probably a random prank, but you need to be careful anyway." Liam looked solemnly at his wife, making sure his words sank in.

"I know. I was already thinking the same thing. Maybe the ballet studio has video cameras outside that might have picked it up? It wasn't even dark when I parked the car there. I can't believe someone would be brazen enough to do that in broad daylight. I'm scared, Liam. Do you think someone's after me again?" She looked at her husband for the answers she so desperately needed.

The strange occurrences were starting to add up. Emma thought about the things that happened in the past few weeks, most of which she hadn't revealed to Liam. They could all simply be coincidences and products of her overactive imagination, but when she added them to her slashed tires, it was worrisome. Considering what she'd gone through with Xavier, she was concerned.

"Nothing is going to happen to you, Emma. You're safe with me. I won't let anyone hurt you ever again." Liam tipped her face up to his. "Trust me."

"I do trust you, Liam. I trust you with my life. For better

or for worse. But thank goodness for Morgan. She's turning out to be a great friend."

"Maybe you were right about her after all." Liam grabbed his phone to call the tow truck.

TWENTY-TWO

The next day, Liam watched the tire repairman remove all four tires from Emma's SUV. The two men examined them, both coming to the same conclusion.

"I hate to tell you this, Mr. O'Reilly, but in my opinion, it was done on purpose." Al, the tire man, scratched his head as he spoke. "Someone used a razor blade on each one."

"That's what I was afraid of. Have you had any more cars brought in for the same thing? Sometimes kids go on a vandalism spree and hit several at once." Liam was hopeful that was the case. He wanted to believe it was a senseless act by a teenage vandal.

"Can't say I have. This is the only one I've seen, anyway."

"All right, thanks, Al. Go ahead and replace them. Call me when it's finished." Liam shook Al's hand and headed back to his Mustang.

Driving across town, the wheels were turning in his head as fast as they were rotating on his car. He didn't like it one bit. Sure, it could be an isolated prank, and Emma was just a random victim. Things like that certainly happened. Something in his gut told him otherwise, though. Coupled with the fact that he recently had to install surveillance cameras in the alley behind Morning Glory because of Emma's encounter with graffiti, the latest incident didn't sit well with him.

Liam reminded himself that this was Beckland, not Chicago. More than likely, these were two isolated events, and Emma was just unlucky to be victim of both. Sometimes the things Liam had seen over the course of his career clouded his opinion of humanity. He always assumed the worst, and that was just part of the job. It didn't make him irrational. When it came to Emma, though, his protective nature took over his logical, analytical mind, and all he saw was danger lurking everywhere.

He knew he tended to overreact and probably smothered her a bit, but he couldn't help it. After what happened with Xavier, he couldn't be too careful. Emma didn't know it, but he called the prison and got an update on Xavier once a week. He wanted to be absolutely certain that the monster was securely locked behind prison doors for a good long time.

Pulling up in front of Beckland Ballet Academy, Liam greeted Kelly, the receptionist, with a smile. She was familiar with him because he was often the one who brought Lily to class. He needed to see if the academy had video cameras outside. He was hoping he might get lucky and find out who slashed Emma's tires.

Kelly listened to the problem and told him she was more than happy to let him watch the tapes from their video cameras. He followed her to the back room, where she gave him complete access to the security system. He thanked her and she returned to the front desk.

Liam settled himself into a chair and rewound the tapes to yesterday at the time Emma parked the car. He watched intently as their SUV pulled up to the building, Lily dashed in, and Emma searched for a parking space. Instead of going into the studio, Emma strolled away into town.

He watched for several more minutes, but nothing relevant happened. Liam glanced at the timer on the tape and realized he had been staring at cars sitting in the parking lot for thirty minutes. He ran his hands through his hair in frustration, then fast-forwarded the tape, frame by frame, suddenly hitting Stop as he saw it.

He watched a figure approach Emma's parked vehicle and walk around it twice while casting furtive glances all around. The figure bent down at every tire before walking away at a casual pace.

The tape was crystal clear, which should have meant that he'd hit the jackpot. Unfortunately, the person was in disguise. The figure was clothed in all black, in a large puffy black jacket with the hood pulled closely, obscuring any facial features. Given the way the culprit was covered in layers, Liam couldn't tell how large or small the person really was. The only thing he could gauge was height, and he had the suspect pegged at about five eight or five nine. That wasn't a lot to go on, so he re-watched several more times, hoping to notice something he hadn't before. Much to his dismay, he didn't.

He set the tape to the current time, turned it back on, and thanked Kelly as he left.

TWENTY-THREE

Jumping in his car, Liam hit the gas and drove toward the Beckland police station. He was going to run the situation by a couple of his friends there and see if they could offer a fresh perspective. If Liam had learned one thing over the years, it was the fact that sometimes you were just too close to a case to see it clearly. A fresh pair of eyes was sometimes enough to make the pieces move into place.

He was aware that he wasn't at all objective when it came to Emma, so he probably needed an outsider's opinion. He now knew for sure that someone had purposely slashed Emma's tires. He'd seen it on camera with his own eyes. What he didn't know was whether or not there was enough evidence to conclude that she was in danger, or if it was merely a harmful prank. One way or another, he was going to find out.

An hour later, after a lengthy discussion with some of Beckland's finest, he walked into the parking lot, still trying to convince himself that Emma was in no danger. He'd told the officers the entire story, not leaving anything out. While they admitted that the two instances were frustrating, they didn't see enough evidence to support the theory that Emma was in any kind of grave danger. They came to the conclusion that the circumstances were unrelated, and that Liam and Emma should just put it behind them and move on to happier things, like the upcoming birth of their daughter.

While Liam respected the opinions of the officers, something still didn't sit right with him.

He started his car and drove away from the police station. He stopped at the stop sign and noticed his brakes seemed a little worn out. His Mustang was due for a tune-up, and he made a mental note to make an appointment with Al when he called to let them know Emma's vehicle was fixed.

Rather than head home, Liam needed to pay a visit to the Warfield courthouse to take a look at some records he needed for a case he was working on. The girls were at school, Emma was at work, and if he didn't waste any time, he would be home to make dinner.

Heading out of town, he turned onto County Road 15. It was a beautiful day for a drive, and Liam accelerated, enjoying the sound his car made as it shifted smoothly between gears. It was a winding road, and Liam loved the way the Mustang hugged the curves.

Glancing down at the speedometer, he realized he was going a little too fast for the curve that was ahead. When he pressed his foot down to apply the brakes, the pedal went all the way to the floorboard. Liam pumped the brake pedal again, but the car still didn't slow down. In fact, the momentum he had built up on the downhill descent sent the car speeding out of control.

Trying not to panic, Liam pulled the emergency brake, realizing he was in trouble. It had no impact on the speeding vehicle, and the Mustang continued to gain velocity.

Liam assessed the situation and, seeing no other cars on the road, made a split-second decision. He aimed for the side of the road, knowing it was the only way to avoid hitting a potential oncoming car.

Liam felt the car bump and thud as it stalled, left the pavement, and met the grassy bank on the side of the road. As the tree loomed in front of him, his last conscious thought was to brace for the impending impact.

The last thing he heard was the crunch of metal as it came in contact with the tree.

TWENTY-FOUR

Arriving home from work, Emma reveled in the fact that she had the house to herself for a while. Time alone was such a rare treat that she intended to take advantage of it. She prepared a cup of tea, grabbed the book she wanted to begin, and basked in the blessed silence.

She'd no sooner settled into the first chapter when there was a knock at the door. Wondering who it could be, she opened it, completely unprepared for what was waiting on the other side. The police officers standing there caused her to flash back to the day she was told of Jacob's death more than seven years before. She'd been pregnant then, as well.

The officers provided little information, telling her in hushed voices that Liam had been in a terrible car accident and was currently unconscious. Knowing she had to get to him immediately, she asked them to alert Sadie that she needed her to stay with the girls when they got home from school. One officer did as she asked, and the other drove the terrified mother to the hospital, lights flashing to clear their path.

Emma was completely out of breath as she ran down the

corridor of the Beckland Community Hospital emergency room. She held her bulging stomach, her lungs burning as she ran blindly in the direction the nurses had instructed.

Tears streamed down her face. She was frantic to get to Liam. The feeling of doom surrounding her was so tangible that she could feel its death grip. She stopped in front of the room where Liam was and took a deep breath before entering. She had no idea what she might find, and she steeled herself for the worst.

Emma opened the door and walked inside. There was Liam, bruised, bloody, and unconscious. Her hands fluttered to her lips to cover the gasp she was unable to stifle. Her strong, invincible husband lay helpless in the hospital bed, not even aware of her presence.

With trepidation, she went to his side and pulled the chair as close to the bed as she could manage. Gingerly, she clasped his bandaged hand in hers and felt the connection between them like an electric current. She willed her strength and love into him, not really knowing what else to do.

She prayed and pleaded with God. She begged Him for help, unsure what she was even praying for at that point, other than that Liam wouldn't die. She didn't know the extent of his injuries, but it appeared he had many. She anxiously waited for a doctor or nurse to come in and answer her questions.

After what seemed like an interminable amount of time, there was a slight knock at the door and the doctor entered. To her amazement and relief, it was Dr. Woods, the doctor who had attended her after Xavier's attack. She was an amazing and caring doctor, and Emma knew Liam was in good hands.

"Emma, I'm so sorry we're meeting again for this reason. I know you must be worried sick about your husband, but I'm also worried about you. You must keep your anxiety under control to ensure your blood pressure remains in the safe zone for your baby's sake." Dr. Woods reached out and took Emma's arm, concentrating while she checked her pulse rate.

"I'm fine, just please tell me what's going on with Liam. I don't have any idea what his injuries are. No one has told me anything," she pleaded as she pulled her arm away.

"Well, Emma, it was a very bad accident. Liam has a broken arm and a fractured clavicle. He has extensive bruising on most of his body as well." Dr. Woods looked at her, gauging her reaction as she spoke. "He also has a concussion."

"Why is he unconscious? Does he have brain injuries, too? I know you don't want me to be upset, but give it to me straight, please. I need to know." Emma met her eyes with determination.

"He's sedated. When the ambulance brought him in, he was… uncooperative. He didn't want to be examined, and he kept saying he needed to get to you. Once the adrenaline wore off, however, he passed out from what was obviously an extreme amount of pain. We gave him a sedative to keep him asleep so we were able to work on his injuries."

"Oh my."

"As you well know, Liam is stubborn and strong, and no doubt would have hobbled right out of the ER if we hadn't taken the choice away from him. His arm needed to be set, and he'll have to be on bed rest for several days, but the sedative will wear off and he'll be awake soon."

"So he's going to be okay?" Emma hoped she'd understood correctly.

"Yes, Emma, he's going to be just fine, eventually. He does have broken bones and will be in quite a lot of pain over the next couple of weeks, but I have every confidence that he'll recover nicely. There won't be permanent damage, although I'm not sure how he walked away from this, to be honest with you. The officers at the scene of the crash said it was nothing short of a miracle that he's alive."

Emma let the words sink in. It was a miracle he was alive. The thought that she could have so easily lost Liam was incomprehensible.

"Thank you so much, Dr. Woods," Emma said as the tears began to flow freely again.

"You're welcome, Emma. I'm glad the news was good." Dr. Woods patted Emma's shoulder and smiled as she left the room, assuring her that Liam would wake up before long.

She sat there looking at her husband, a thousand thoughts and feelings flooding her at once. He was going to recover. She kept repeating that to herself, not yet fully believing it. Emma couldn't even fathom what she would do if something were to happen to Liam. He was her rock, and their family needed him like they needed air to breathe. She said a grateful prayer of thanks that he was going to make it.

Wiping the tears from her face, she tried to gain some control over her fragile emotions. She needed to be strong.

About that time, Liam's eyes fluttered open and his face filled with confusion. He looked around, obviously trying to figure out where he was.

"Emma?" He searched her eyes for answers.

"Hey, sleepyhead." She smiled into his blue eyes. "You're all right. You were in an accident. Do you remember?"

"Not really. I remember… bits and pieces. I was driving… and I tried to put on the brakes… but nothing happened." Liam's words and thoughts were a jumble as he tried to piece his memories together. "I remember I needed to get to you."

"You're fine. Just relax," she said soothingly. His agitation was rising, and he was twisting around in bed. Knowing him, he would be trying to break out of there any minute.

"Emma, someone did this on purpose. Probably the same person who slashed your tires. The police are mistaken if they think this is all a coincidence." Liam's eyes were hard as steel, and she knew it was her job to keep him calm.

"I'm sure you're right. You usually are. The important thing right now is that you need to rest. We can figure it all out once you're feeling better. Liam, your arm and collarbone are both broken, and you're pretty much bruised from head to toe. You aren't going anywhere for a few days." She tried to give him the facts without riling him further.

Liam muttered something under his breath, and she didn't ask him to clarify. She was probably better off not knowing. The only thing that mattered was keeping him relaxed and in the hospital bed where he belonged. Knowing how obstinate he was, it was going to be a full-time job.

"I'm sorry to put you through this. I know you must have been terrified when they told you I was in an accident." Liam reached for her hand.

"That's an understatement. It was like déjà vu when the police officers showed up at the house. I was so afraid I was going to lose you, Liam." She tried to keep her emotions in check, but saying the words out loud was more than she could stand. She started crying again.

"Hey, I'm not going anywhere anytime soon. You can't get rid of me that easily." Liam smiled, then winced from the pain of the lacerations on his face.

"I'm going to hold you to that. I'm counting on you not to leave me," she said, wiping the tears.

"I'll never leave you, Emma." Liam squeezed her hand and settled into the hospital bed. He had no other choice but to accept his confinement.

TWENTY-FIVE

Liam was kept in the emergency room the rest of the night for observation. Emma called Sadie to check in and was told the girls were very worried, but they were holding up well. Knowing Emma wouldn't be leaving Liam's side, Sadie assured her friend that she would stay with them for as long as it was needed. Emma was so thankful for Sadie; she knew their friendship was something rare.

She said good night to each of her daughters over the phone, calming their fears and telling them to be good for Sadie. After that, she called Jane to let her know what was going on. Jane said not to worry about anything except Liam, and told her things were under control at Morning Glory. She also promised she would try not to fire Morgan while Emma was gone.

She didn't think she was going to get any rest, but that didn't matter. She needed to be close to Liam. Pulling the chair next to his bed, she tried to find a good position. Sleeping in a hospital chair was never a comfortable option, but attempting to do so at nearly eight months pregnant was practically impossible. Every position was more uncomfortable than the last.

Liam was sleeping well, mostly because of the pain medication, but Emma was wide awake and her muscles were screaming. There was another chair in the corner, so she pulled it over and placed her aching, swollen feet onto it.

After an hour or so of squirming, she finally settled into a position that didn't have her groaning. She eventually fell asleep, waking frequently throughout the night, a couple of times to use the bathroom and a couple more to be sure Liam was still all right. When morning arrived, she was not well-rested in the least.

The morning shift doctor came in and checked Liam, informing them that he was happy with the way the injuries looked. Liam was officially admitted into the hospital and moved to a room on the second floor. The nurses on that floor were gracious and kind, and they must have taken pity on Emma, because they brought in a cot. She tested it out, and while it was not the most comfortable arrangement by any stretch of the imagination, it was worlds better than the chair-bed she'd rigged up the night before. It was a small thing, but she was grateful.

Liam arrived in his room just in time to place his breakfast order, and he added some for Emma as well. She was desperate for a shower, but it didn't look like that was going to happen. She wasn't ready to leave Liam, even for the promise of bathing.

"How are you holding up?" Liam asked from his bed. "I know you want to be with me, but you have to think of yourself and the baby too. Sleeping in a chair isn't really a feasible option for you right now, Em."

"Well I won't be in a chair tonight, will I? The nurses brought in the cot, so I'll be sleeping in the lap of luxury." She smiled at her worrisome husband to let him know she was just fine.

"I'm aware of the cot. That doesn't really cut it for a woman who is only weeks away from giving birth." Liam was stubborn, but he was no match for his wife.

"Let me ask you this, Liam," she challenged. "If the roles were reversed and I was the one in the hospital bed, would you go home to sleep?"

"Of course not! I wouldn't leave your side," Liam said passionately.

"Exactly! You have your answer, then, don't you?" She knew he had no room to argue with her logic.

"I guess I do," he conceded.

"So let's just let that conversation rest, okay? I'm not leaving, and that's final." She kissed him on the cheek.

"I love you so much, Emma. All I could think about when they were pulling me out of the car yesterday was that it might have been you. None of the things that have happened are a coincidence. They're all connected, I just haven't figured out how. I'm more worried than ever that you're in danger." Liam gripped her hand with his good one.

"From the looks of things, we're both in danger. After all, you're the one in the hospital bed right now. We just need to focus on getting you healed and ready to go home."

Her gut told her Liam was right about the danger, but she couldn't allow herself to think about it. If she did, she would go back to the way she was a few months before, fearful of her own shadow. Liam needed her to be strong for him, not a cowering victim.

They watched television until breakfast arrived. Right after they finished eating, Lieutenant Jones from the Beckland police department came into the room. From the look on his face, Emma knew he wasn't there on a social call.

"Lieutenant Jones," Liam said. "What brings you here?"

"I wanted to check on you, first of all. I'm sure glad you're going to be all right," the police officer said awkwardly.

"Thanks, but what's the real reason you're paying me a visit today?" Liam cut straight to the point.

"Well." Lieutenant Jones shifted from foot to foot as he tried to formulate his words. "I don't know how to tell you this, Liam, but your car accident was no accident."

"I could have told you that. In fact, I think I alluded to the idea that our family was in danger only minutes before I plowed into that tree." Liam's blue eyes turned cold as he looked at the officer.

"You were right. We should have taken the threat much more seriously, and I apologize that we didn't. We determined that your emergency brake line was cut completely, and there was a puncture in your main brake line, which eventually caused complete brake system failure. Obviously this was done on purpose. We're attempting to tie this together with Emma's tires being slashed, as well as the graffiti incident at Morning Glory. I just wanted you to know that we're looking into it." He looked relieved that he had gotten his speech out of the way.

"Well I appreciate you looking into it, Lieutenant, but you'll forgive me if I don't put a lot of stock in your investigative skills. I'm well aware the Beckland police force doesn't have the manpower needed to launch a full investigation, so you'll pardon me when I tell you that I will be conducting my own investigation as well." Liam's response to the officer was delivered in a voice that was full of determination.

Lieutenant Jones looked a little nervous. Liam was calling in the Feds, after all. One of their own was a target.

"I assumed you would do just that, Liam. I wouldn't expect otherwise. Anyhow, I just wanted to check in on you. I hope you get out of here soon. Let us know if you come across any new information." He nodded curtly as he left the room.

Emma sat in silence as she processed what she'd just heard. Liam's brake lines had been tampered with. Someone had purposely cut the lines in an attempt to hurt and potentially kill her husband. While her tires being slashed hadn't put her life in jeopardy, it was definitely a warning. Add in the gruesome doll, the strange car driving past the coffee shop, and the graffiti at Morning Glory, and it was enough to let her know that something was very wrong.

"Liam, I'm worried. Someone is clearly trying to send us a message. Do you think it's Xavier?" she asked the question that had plagued her since the first incident occurred.

"I don't think it's Xavier directly, but he may be involved. He's safe behind bars where he belongs, but I'm sure his cronies are out there. You can be sure that a guy like Xavier has built up a list of associates over the years."

Emma tried to keep the fear from her face, and for the most part, she was holding it together fairly well. She was terrified, and her first thought was for the safety of Sadie and the girls. Liam must have read her mind.

"I'm going to call the police station and ask them to post an officer outside the house for now. I don't want to scare Sadie and the girls, but I want to be sure they're safe while I'm stuck here." Liam asked her to get his phone and dial the station.

While he talked, Emma grabbed her own phone and stepped out into the hall. She needed to call Sadie and let her know what was going on. She had to warn her to be extra careful, and not to let the girls out of her sight, even for a second. She also wanted her friend to know that she shouldn't be alarmed to see a police car outside of the house.

In Sadie-like fashion, she took the phone call in stride. It seemed nothing in the world could rattle Emma's steady best friend. She trusted Sadie completely to care for her daughters. Sadie would keep them safe.

When she went back into the room, it was clear that the conversation with the police precinct hadn't gone well. Liam told her they agreed to place an officer at their house for two days, but couldn't spare the manpower any longer than that.

Liam's injuries were going to keep him in the hospital for at least four days, so that meant Sadie and the girls would be left unprotected for two days. Realistically, even after Liam went home, he was going to be out of commission for a while. She wasn't sure what they were going to do.

"I have a plan. You just need to trust me. I'm going to take care of our family, Emma." Liam reached out and grabbed her hand. "I need to make another phone call. If the Beckland police won't protect us, then I'll pull in my own resources."

Emma knew Liam would take care of things, so she left him to it. She needed some time alone to digest the facts that had been brought to light. She told Liam she was going to take a walk around the hallways, but promised she wouldn't leave the floor; she just wanted to stretch her legs and process all of the emotions that she felt.

Deep down, Emma was terrified. The problem was she had no idea who she was afraid of. The logical assumption was that Xavier was pulling strings from prison. Maybe he was out to get revenge on them for putting him there. On the other hand, it might be someone else who was connected to Emma's ex-husband and his mistress and their ring of jewelry thieves. There were lots of people who had been wronged by them, and it would be easy for someone like that to come after her family out of spite.

She paced the hallways, knowing she had to keep her fear in check. She couldn't get stressed or upset, or she would end up in the hospital along with Liam when her blood pressure skyrocketed. Emma's daughters and husband needed her to be strong, and that's what she was going to do.

Filled with a new sense of purpose, she headed back to Liam's room.

"Feel better?" Liam asked as she sat down beside him.

"I do. Everything is going to be just fine. We're a great team, and we'll figure this all out together." She hoped she sounded more convincing than she felt.

"Well, our team is about to get a little bit bigger. I just got off the phone with my cousin. He'll be getting on a plane today and coming to stay with us for a while." Liam smiled, but Emma could hear the determination in his voice. He had obviously made a decision and set it into motion, all within the last few minutes.

"Your cousin? I'm guessing this isn't a cousin I've met," she ventured.

"His name is Colin, and he lives in Ireland. Our fathers are brothers. When Mom and Dad moved to the United States, Colin's dad stayed there. Colin is an ex-police officer who now works as a private detective. He's wanted to visit, and now is as good a time as any. He'll stay with us indefinitely, and the good news is that he's more than happy to help me with the investigation and security detail."

Liam sounded relieved to have come up with an answer to their problem, and it seemed like a perfect solution. Emma was excited to meet another member of his family, and it would take some of the pressure off Liam so he could recover properly.

They spent the rest of the day watching daytime talk shows and wishing they were anywhere but there. The doctor came in late that afternoon and told Liam he would get to go home two days later. It was sooner than expected, and Liam was happy with the news.

The couple ate dinner together and settled in for another

long night in the hospital. As Emma lay down on her cot that night, she gave thanks that Liam was doing well, and that they had a solution to their problem. She wondered what Colin would be like. She couldn't wait to meet him.

Emma closed her eyes and drifted into a dreamless sleep, missing her daughters, yet glad she would be home soon.

TWENTY-SIX

THREE DAYS LATER, LIAM AND EMMA STOOD AT BAGGAGE claim at the Columbus International Airport. Liam had been sent home the day before, with instructions to rest. That was easier said than done. He was in a full arm cast, as well as a sling to keep his arm stable to allow his collarbone to heal properly. He was bruised and sore, but seemed to be getting along fairly well, all things considered.

He'd insisted on making the two-hour drive from Beckland to Columbus to retrieve Colin, even though Emma told him he should stay home and sleep. Honestly, she was glad he'd decided to come. She'd never laid eyes on Colin and had no idea what he looked like.

Emma soon discovered that she needn't have worried, because she could have spotted Colin anywhere. He was the spitting image of Liam. They couldn't have looked more alike if they were twins. The only difference was the fact that Colin's hair was a shade lighter, and it was cut shorter. Other than that, they were the same height, build, and even shared the same shade of blue eyes. There were obviously some strong genes in the O'Reilly pool.

"Liam, what's the story?" Colin approached and engulfed Liam in a gentle bear hug.

His accent was thick and charming, and Emma knew immediately that she would never tire of hearing it. The sound was just like music. It might take some time to decipher all the words, but she wouldn't mind.

"Colin, good to see you. I'm so glad you're here." Liam pumped his cousin's hand up and down briskly with his good one. "I'd like you to meet my wife. This is Emma."

"Emma, 'tis nice meetin' ya. Liam, my boy, you hit the jackpot with this one." Colin smiled, and Emma thought it wasn't fair for all that handsomeness to run in one family. The O'Reilly men certainly had the market cornered on good looks and charm.

"We are so glad you're here, Colin. We hope you'll stay with us for a while." Emma hugged him and welcomed him to the United States.

They gathered his bags and headed to the parking garage to make the two-hour drive home. Liam and Colin chatted about old times, and then Liam brought him up to speed on the problems they were having. The men threw around theories and ideas, brainstormed ways to keep the family safe, and basically "talked shop." Emma was happy to let them catch up, and she drove along quietly, taking it all in.

Arriving home at dusk, they unloaded Colin's bags from the SUV. Emma was happy her vehicle was fixed, but Liam hadn't been so lucky with his Mustang. It was completely totaled, so they were down to a single car until he bought a new one.

"We're home!" Emma called out as they walked through the front door.

"The girls are in the kitchen. I'll be right down," Sadie called from upstairs.

The group walked through the foyer and into the kitchen.

Liam introduced Colin to the girls, and Emma could see their amazement as they noticed the resemblance between their father and his cousin.

"Wow. You look like our dad!" Dahlia stated the obvious.

"That we do, Dahlia. The craic was mighty when we were young. We looked so much alike that we fooled folks often," Colin laughed.

"Craic?" Lily asked.

"Fun," Colin clarified.

"I like the way you talk," Rose said shyly.

"Sure, an' I like the way you talk." Colin smiled and Rose blushed.

"Hey, guys, I made some dinner." Sadie sailed into the room and stopped dead in her tracks when she spotted Colin.

The two stared at one another and the electricity practically crackled between them, rushing like a current. Emma smiled to herself. What an interesting turn of events! She hadn't even thought of Colin as a possible interest for Sadie, but from their reactions, it looked like that might be in the works.

"Sadie, this is my cousin, Colin. Colin, this is Emma's best friend, Sadie Ross. She lives upstairs," Liam explained, but Emma doubted that either of them heard a word.

"Ta tu go h-alainn," Colin said, almost under his breath.

"I'm sorry, what did you say?" Sadie stepped closer to Colin.

"I said, 'you're beautiful.' It's Gaelic," Colin answered quietly.

"Oh, thank you. That… was, uh… beautifully said," Sadie stammered.

Confident, self-assured Sadie appeared to be frazzled. Emma had never seen her friend so completely out of her element, and she was curious to see what would happen next.

"Can we eat? I'm hungry," Rose unceremoniously interrupted the mood.

"Of course, Rosie! The girls and I made some homemade chicken noodle soup. It's such a cold night, and it sounded like a cozy dish to warm us all up." Sadie snapped back to reality and walked to the stove, busying herself with finishing up the meal.

Liam and Emma shared a knowing look. Neither had missed the fireworks display between Sadie and Colin. Emma could tell Liam was just as surprised by it as she was. Colin, who seemed to be riveted in place, continued to watch Sadie, even though her back was now turned to them.

"Let's all sit down, shall we?" Emma attempted to break the spell that had fallen over Colin by taking his arm and leading him to his place at the table. He still hadn't said a word.

Liam sat beside Colin, and Emma went to the stove to help Sadie, whose wide eyes met hers. She could relate. Emma knew firsthand what it felt like to experience that "knock you off your feet" attraction to an O'Reilly man. Sadie didn't stand a chance.

"You okay?" Emma asked quietly.

"Emma... what... I mean... wow... er... I have... no words," Sadie stammered.

"I see that." Emma laughed.

"He's gorgeous, and that accent... and the Gaelic... and... yeah," Sadie responded breathlessly, and Emma thought for a moment that her friend might actually swoon.

"You'll be fine. If not, I'll break out the smelling salts. By the way, he hasn't stopped staring at you since you came over here." Emma giggled as Sadie glanced over her shoulder.

"My hands are shaking so badly that I'll probably spill the soup all over him." Sadie rolled her eyes as she carried the serving dish to the table where everyone was seated.

It was a very quiet meal, full of stolen, furtive glances between Colin and Sadie. Colin's obvious infatuation didn't dampen his appetite, and he practically inhaled three bowls of Sadie's soup. Sadie, on the other hand, swirled her soup around in her bowl but didn't take a single bite. Liam and Emma watched, amused at the two of them. The only ones talking were the girls, chattering amongst themselves, seemingly unaware of the drama being played out between the adults.

When they finished eating, Colin and Liam said they would clean up the kitchen, and the women didn't argue. Emma instructed the girls to start their bedtime routine, so she and Sadie headed to the living room, anxious to talk a bit more in private.

It wasn't long before Sadie said she needed to go home and get some sleep. Emma walked her to the front door. Emma doubted sleep would come easily for her best friend, but she didn't say so. Colin must have been waiting, because the moment they reached the door, he was there.

"'Twas lovely to meet ya," Colin said with a smile.

Sadie's cheeks turned a bright shade of red. "You too, Colin." She extended her hand, but instead of shaking it, Colin drew it close to his lips and gently kissed it. She looked as if she might pass out.

"Will ya be a'right walkin' home alone?" Colin asked.

"It's just upstairs, but you can escort me if you'd like," Sadie answered with a shy smile.

"Sure, I think I will." Colin helped Sadie into her coat, and the two of them disappeared out the front door.

"Well, that certainly didn't take long." Emma laughed while she recounted the tale to Liam as he finished loading the dishwasher. "I've known Sadie all my life, and I've never seen her react to anyone like that before."

"I have to say, I didn't see that coming, although it's not

really surprising. Colin couldn't do better than Sadie, that's for sure," Liam replied.

"I suppose we shouldn't jump to conclusions and marry them off yet, but wouldn't it be perfect if they ended up together?" Emma clapped her hands and squealed with delight as Liam laughed at his wife's reaction.

A few minutes later, Colin returned. His face was flushed and he was wearing a dreamy smile. He hadn't bothered with a coat, so the rosiness in his cheeks might have been from the cold evening, but Emma had her suspicions that it had more to do with Sadie.

"Thanks for walking Sadie home, Colin." Emma smiled broadly.

"'Twas my pleasure. She's a lovely woman. Sorry I abandoned you with the cleanup, Liam," Colin replied a bit sheepishly.

Once the kitchen was spotlessly scrubbed, they showed Colin to the room that would be his. He was clearly exhausted after the long flight, not to mention the excitement of meeting Sadie.

Liam and Emma told him good night, tucked the girls in, and retired to their room for the evening. As Emma lay in bed, she smiled at the unexpected way the night had gone. Liam wanted Colin there to help him watch out for their family, but Emma had a feeling that his most important purpose might be something entirely different.

TWENTY-SEVEN

THE NEXT FEW DAYS PASSED BENIGNLY, AND GIVEN THE circumstances, that was just fine with the O'Reilly clan. Uneventfulness was safe. Liam and Colin worked together to come up with a security plan for the household, which also included Sadie. Everyone had strict instructions not to leave the house alone, without exception. That meant Colin drove the girls to school and picked them up each day, since Liam wasn't yet able to drive. Sadie and Emma were both escorted to and from work as well.

Emma knew it was all a matter of safety, and she appreciated the effort. Still, she couldn't help being a little frustrated by the fact that she was once again in a situation that required her constant surveillance. Sadie, on the other hand, didn't seem to mind it one bit, as Colin always volunteered to see her safely to work and back each day. They were becoming quite comfortable with each other, and that pleased both Liam and Emma. Something positive had grown out of something negative.

Liam and Colin discussed their "situation" in hushed tones, so Emma knew very little about the investigation. It was irritating to her. She didn't really want to know the details, but she didn't like living in constant fear of the unknown. When she asked Liam about it, he just said that he and Colin were hard at work, trying to make sense of what little information they had. He assured his wife that she was safe and nothing would happen to any of them.

While she knew it was true, Emma couldn't help feeling on edge. She was like a bird in a cage, and all she wanted was some freedom to fly. Liam consoled her by saying it wouldn't last forever, and she just needed to hang in there and trust him.

By the second week of Operation Babysitter, Emma had enough. She was tired of being worried about her own safety, and she felt completely smothered. She was more than eight months pregnant, and in a few short weeks, she'd be tied down with an infant. She wanted to embrace her freedom while she had it. That was something the men in her life couldn't understand.

So, when Morgan suggested a spur-of-the-moment shopping trip to Warfield Mall, Emma wholeheartedly agreed. A day of fun and girl talk was exactly what she needed. Emma wanted to ask Sadie to join them, but she knew her cautious best friend would side with Liam and say they shouldn't go. As much as Emma wanted to include her, she kept her mouth shut.

Liam would never approve, so she didn't tell him either. That morning, Emma prepared for work as usual, planning to leave with Morgan after Liam walked her next door. It was Morgan's day off, and she was driving. Emma hated being underhanded with Liam, but she really needed to get away for just a few hours. She would be back before the girls got off the bus, and no one would be the wiser.

Dressing for work, Emma went to the laundry room to grab her maternity jeans out of the dryer. She noticed Liam's pocketknife was lying on the floor, so she picked it up and put it in her pocket, thinking she would give it to him later. The man was forever leaving things in his pockets, which then ended up in the laundry. One time, she even washed his cell phone. It clearly hadn't taught him the lesson of emptying his pockets before the items hit the dirty clothes hamper.

An hour later, Liam walked her to work and she kissed him goodbye, feeling a momentary twinge of guilt that she wasn't being completely honest. She contemplated telling him about her plans. It felt wrong to keep things from him, but she knew he would never agree. Emma wasn't up for an argument, so she kept it to herself.

Pushing down the guilt, she told herself that she deserved a day of fun. She informed Jane about the shopping trip, but also reminded her of the fact that no one knew she was going. She seemed a little worried, but told Emma to do what she needed to. Jane looked uncomfortable as she waved goodbye. Emma hoped Liam stayed busy with work and didn't decide to pop into Morning Glory for a coffee and ask Jane where she was.

Emma felt a sense of glorious independence as she and Morgan sped out of Beckland in the woman's black sports car. She had the next few hours to herself, and she didn't even care what they did. They could just drive around all day and that would be fine. It was freeing to not be part of someone's "security detail." Emma noticed Morgan was uncharacteristically quiet, and she wondered if her friend might be a little nervous about breaking the rules. Emma tried to make small talk, but Morgan didn't have much to say.

That was fine with Emma. She was simply enjoying the ride in Morgan's fancy car. It was certainly luxurious, and she couldn't imagine being able to afford a car like that. She didn't know the model, but she knew it was rare. Emma remembered seeing another car like it once, but for the life of her, she couldn't remember where. Emma's brain was so foggy these days; she blamed the pregnancy hormones.

The women were about thirty minutes into their forty-five-minute drive to Warfield when Morgan asked Emma if she wanted something to drink. Emma said she did, so Morgan pulled into a diner along the road. Emma's legs were starting to cramp, and she tried to adjust herself in the seat. Morgan suggested that Emma might want to stretch her legs, so she went inside to get their drinks. Emma asked for hot tea with honey, and Morgan said she'd be back soon.

Five minutes later, Morgan returned, drinks in hand. They climbed back into the car and drove a little farther. Fall was making way for winter, and the chilling November winds were blowing. The sky was gray, and the promise of rain was in the air. A lot of folks found the fall to be dull and depressing, but Emma loved it.

Sipping her hot tea, Emma settled back into the plush leather seat of Morgan's car and looked out the window. The hot, sweet liquid was relaxing.

Out of nowhere, Emma remembered that day in the alley when she'd thought she was being watched. Like a movie replaying in her mind, Emma saw it happening in slow motion. Emma recalled the black, fancy sports car slowing down at the end of the street, her knowledge that the driver was watching her, even though she couldn't see clearly through the darkly tinted glass. Emma knew with sudden certainty where she'd seen the other car like Morgan's, though it seemed a rather strange coincidence.

They were only about fifteen minutes away from Warfield, and as Emma watched the trees and grass speed by, she suddenly felt dizzy. She placed her head on the headrest and blinked a few times. She'd battled vertigo during her pregnancy, and she knew it would pass.

Blinking again, Emma noticed that her eyelids weighed a thousand pounds. It took a tremendous amount of effort to open them each time they closed. She desperately wanted to sleep. She lifted her head as another wave of dizziness washed over her. Emma's body was floating, and her fingers were tingly. She turned her head to look at Morgan, but everything was moving in slow motion. It was a dreamlike state, and when Emma tried to speak, her voice sounded like it was underwater.

"It was you." Emma thought she said the words to Morgan, but she couldn't be sure.

Emma felt herself slip deeper and deeper into the blackness, unable to form words at all. She was just so tired. Her brain was screaming, "Wake up, Emma," but her body wanted nothing more than to give in to the promise of blissful sleep.

In the end, her body won the war, and the last thing Emma remembered before closing her eyes was Morgan's chilling smile.

TWENTY-EIGHT

EMMA WAS FLOATING, BLISSFULLY BUOYANT IN THE WATER. SHE looked at her arms, chubby and childlike, encased in the pink-flowered floaties her mama insisted she wear. Her short, little girl legs kicked in the water, happy and excited to be swimming.

Emma's mom stood close by, smiling proudly as her little girl mastered the butterfly stroke she'd been teaching her. Emma hoped her mother would allow her to remove the arm floats. She'd pleaded with her all summer, but her mother refused, telling Emma she wasn't yet ready. Her mother clapped and laughed as Emma swam, a look of pure joy on her beautiful face. Emma was happy she'd finally learned. They'd worked together on the skill for weeks.

Emma's mom kept telling her daughter that when it was time to take off the safety gear, they would both know. Even in Emma's six-year-old mind, she knew the time had come. She'd mastered the lesson, and she was proficient enough to swim on her own, free from the restrictive arm floats.

"I did it, Mama!" Emma laughed as she swam to her mother, wrapping her arms around the woman tightly.

"Yes, you did, Emma. I told you the day was coming." Her

mother pushed the little girl's dripping strawberry blonde ringlets off her forehead.

Out of nowhere, the sky above grew dark and threatening. Gone were the sunlight and the benign, puffy clouds. Thunderheads rolled in. Lightning flashed and the wind roared, and Emma was suddenly frightened. She gripped her mother tightly, but her arms were no longer the arms of a child. Emma was her fully grown adult self, looking to her mother for help.

"Mama, what's happening? I'm so scared." Emma glanced around frantically, confused and unsure of what was going on. "Where are my daughters?"

Panic set in and Emma tried to run, but she was still standing in the water, which had turned dark and frigid. Emma's body trembled and she began to cry, knowing she must do something, but not knowing what.

"Emma, look at me." Her mother grabbed her shoulders, turning her body so she could see nothing but the green of her mother's eyes, so much like her own. "Listen to me. I told you the day was coming. It's here. It's now. Fight with everything inside of you. You are so much stronger than you know."

"But I'm not, Mama," Emma sobbed. "I'm afraid. I don't know what to do. Help me."

"It's time to wake up, Emma. Open your eyes, now," Mama commanded.

HER MOTHER'S FACE DISAPPEARED, AND EMMA OPENED HER eyes. She was in Morgan's car, but it was no longer moving. She had no idea how much time had passed since she'd blacked out, but she had the feeling that she'd been asleep for a while.

Emma turned her head slowly to the left, not sure if she was alone. Morgan was no longer in the driver seat, but the car doors were locked. Frantically taking in her surroundings, she realized she had no idea where she was. It was a secluded road, surrounded on all sides by overgrown trees and bushes.

Up ahead there was a small run-down shack. Emma's brain was aware enough to understand that she was in very real danger, and she had to find a way out. Knowing she must work quickly before Morgan returned, Emma grabbed her purse and dug inside for her cell phone. Her hands shook as she retrieved it, but her hopes were quickly dashed when she saw there was no signal. She tried anyway, but the call she placed to Liam wouldn't go through.

The bushes beside the car began to move, and Emma knew Morgan was returning. She pretended to be asleep in the hope of buying herself some time to come up with a plan.

Morgan slid behind the wheel of the car and drove to the end of the lane. She got out again, fumbling for a set of keys in her purse. Emma opened her eyes enough to watch as the woman unlocked the door of a rickety old shack and disappeared inside. Emma didn't know what was going on, but she was in serious trouble. She could not allow herself to be taken into that shack.

The nausea and dizziness, coupled with the grogginess and blacking out, told Emma that Morgan had drugged her hot tea. She immediately thought of her baby and prayed that whatever drug Morgan used wouldn't cause harm.

Emma thought again of the connection she'd made just before she'd blacked out. As the puzzle pieces took shape in her mind, she knew for sure that Morgan was the reason for all the strange things that had occurred over the past few weeks. Morgan was responsible for the doll, the graffiti, the slashed tires, and Liam's cut brake lines. She had no idea what her motive might be, but she remembered the first day they'd met, months ago, when they'd had the run-in at the mall. The thing that stood out the most in Emma's mind was Morgan's intense anger.

Morgan had told Emma that she would get what she had coming to her. Was this some kind of crazy revenge for bumping into the woman? If so, it was completely disproportionate. It must be tied to something else, but she had no clue what that might be. A million questions buzzed through the fog in Emma's brain, but she couldn't keep up.

Her heart raced. She had to get away.

Grabbing her purse, Emma slowly opened the passenger door and pulled herself to a standing position. She was unsteady on her feet, but she had to take the chance. Ignoring the nausea and dizziness, Emma took a deep breath and made a break for it. Her plan was to head into the woods where she would be harder to find, but at eight months pregnant and under the influence of an unknown substance, she was unable to move quickly.

Morgan didn't have to work very hard to catch up. She came up behind Emma, caught her in a chokehold, and sent her wobbling on her feet. Trying desperately not to lose her balance and fall down, Emma stopped. She didn't fight Morgan, and the woman released her hold on Emma's neck. Instead, she grabbed Emma's arm and pointed a gun to her head.

Emma wanted to run, but she had to think of her baby. The chances of being able to outrun her attacker were nonexistent, and the craziness behind the woman's eyes left no question that she would gladly use the gun if Emma tried to escape.

"Going somewhere, Emma?" Morgan's lovely face contorted into an insane scowl, and Emma thought once again of that day in the mall. She remembered that even though she'd been angry at Morgan, she'd mostly been afraid. As Morgan's true nature was revealed, Emma understood why. Morgan Turner was evil, and Emma had seen it clearly that day.

She'd been fooled by Morgan's act when she came to Beckland. She'd been totally sucked in. Emma inwardly kicked herself, knowing she should have never believed her to be a friend. Everyone had seen right through Morgan—everyone but Emma.

"Morgan, why are you doing this? I thought you were my friend," Emma pleaded as tears of fear and frustration coursed down her face.

"Oh, poor Emma, so used to being loved by everyone. Well, it looks like you should have listened to your friends. I have big plans for you." Morgan's smile was chilling. "Come inside so I can introduce you to your future."

TWENTY-NINE

Morgan shoved Emma through the front door of the old shack, all the while continuing to point the gun at her head. The sight that met her eyes was that of a bleak and desolate prison. Emma's stomach churned in fear, threatening to rid itself of the contents. The wind outside blew swiftly, and the old windows did little to keep it at bay. It whistled through the ancient panes of glass, and the coldness of the room attested to the fact that the cracked windows did little to keep the cold from creeping inside. There was no heat source in the shack, not even a wood stove or fireplace. If the temperature dropped much more, Emma would freeze to death.

The room was completely empty except for a filthy, stained mattress in the corner. There were no blankets or sheets, and the mattress would provide little comfort. There was a rickety wooden chair in the opposite corner, and a small metal table with an ancient record player on top, but that was the extent of furniture in the shack. Next to the disgusting mattress was an old coffee can, and Emma had the horrifying realization that it would serve as her bathroom. The situation was about as dire as it could be.

Emma's gaze returned to the corner with the mattress, and a new sense of desperation set in when she saw the large rope tethered to a metal spike driven deeply into the wooden floor and cemented there. She knew the rope was meant to detain her. Emma's mind raced, trying to come up with a plan. If she tried to fight, she would lose, and Morgan would not hesitate to shoot her. The cold, unfeeling look in the woman's eyes said that she had every intention of killing her. If Emma didn't resist and went along with her, she stood a better chance of either rescue or escape.

Emma allowed herself to be led to the mattress, and Morgan instructed her to get on her knees. Awkwardly, she obeyed. Morgan grabbed the large rope, expertly tied a knot, and wrapped it around Emma's neck. She secured it with a padlock. It hugged Emma's throat tightly and restricted her movement.

Morgan didn't tie Emma's hands or feet, but she couldn't go far in her current state. Emma eased herself into a sitting position on the filthy mattress. She fought the dizziness and nausea, needing to remain alert and ready if an escape route opened.

Morgan walked across the room and sat in the wooden chair. She glared at Emma without saying a word. Finally she laughed, a bone-chilling sound, then turned on the record player. The record crackled, and the voices warbled as they sang an old song that made Emma's blood run cold.

"Goodnight, sweetheart, well it's time to go. Goodnight, sweetheart, well it's time to go. I hate to leave you, but I really must say, goodnight, sweetheart, goodnight."

Under normal circumstances, there was nothing particularly creepy about the song. Emma had heard it many times. However, there was something about Morgan playing it at that moment, coupled with the dead, unfeeling look in the woman's eyes, that told Emma her time was running out. She was so tired, and she wanted nothing more than to collapse onto the dirty mattress. But the rope around her neck reminded her that she couldn't relax. She must find a way out. She was scared and confused, and she had no idea why Morgan had drugged and kidnapped her, but she needed to find out.

"Morgan, why are you doing this? Do you want money? I'll do whatever you want. I'll give you anything. Just let me go," Emma pleaded as the tears flowed freely.

"You really don't get it, do you? You have everything—a husband who's devoted to you, beautiful children, friends who would wage war on your behalf, a gorgeous home, and your own business. You have it all. But that wasn't enough for you, was it? You had to steal the only thing that was mine." Morgan paced back and forth across the creaky floor as the eerie song played in the background.

"Morgan, I don't know what you're talking about. I didn't steal anything from you. I tried to help you. I gave you a job, and I tried to be your friend." She tried her best to sympathize with Morgan, but she couldn't.

"All my life, I wanted a man who would love me for me. Not for my looks, and not for my parents' money. Then I found it. I knew he was the one. He was handsome, rich, and dangerous. I loved him, and I told him so. He'd had a bad relationship, so he was careful. But I knew deep down he loved me."

Morgan was completely engrossed in her tale. Her face was streaked with tears. Suddenly the record player stopped, and so did the story. Emma needed her to keep talking. She had to find out the rest.

"Go on, Morgan," she encouraged.

"Well, he started working on a new job, and little by little he changed. He was engrossed with work. It consumed him. His job was all he thought about. He started taking chances, risking his safety. One night, he made a reckless decision, and it was all over. He ended up in prison." Morgan paused.

"Prison?" Emma breathed the word.

"I'd visit him, tell him I loved him, try to distract him, but it was no use. His heart wasn't mine. You stole it!" Morgan crossed the room.

The deranged woman towered above Emma. Morgan raised her hand and slapped Emma across the face with as much force as she could muster. Emma's head jerked back from the impact, and the rope cinched more tightly around her neck.

In spite of the pain, Emma's brain had begun to process what she was hearing. The puzzle pieces shifted into place. With a sinking heart, Emma asked the question, although she already knew the answer.

"What's his name, Morgan?"

Morgan's eyes were frigid as she bent down and placed her face half an inch from Emma's.

"His name is Xavier."

The name hung in the air between them. Emma's stomach lurched, and she vomited on Morgan's designer boots. Morgan screamed in horror, then punched Emma in the face.

As she began to lose consciousness, she tried to picture Liam's face, but the image wouldn't come.

THIRTY

IT WAS FOUR O'CLOCK IN THE AFTERNOON, AND EMMA WASN'T home. Liam had expected her to call at three thirty so he could walk her home. Colin had already picked up the girls at school, but Emma still hadn't called. He tried not to worry, figuring there might have been an afternoon rush at Morning Glory. At four thirty, he told Colin he was going next door to check on his wife.

Grabbing the rail with his good hand, Liam hobbled down the stairs of the front porch. He walked the short distance to the coffee shop and went inside. To his surprise, the place was empty except for Jane. There was no sign of Emma.

"Hey, Jane, is Emma in her office?" The bad feeling in his gut increased.

"Umm… no… she's not," Jane stammered.

He knew immediately that she was hiding something. "Where is she?" Liam's detective instincts were on full alert. Something wasn't right.

"She's not here." Jane couldn't bring herself to meet his eyes.

"Tell me what's going on, Jane." The grave look on his face left no room for argument.

With a trembling voice, Jane told Liam the whole story. She was relieved to get it off her chest, happy to no longer be harboring a secret. She'd known Emma should have returned by that point, but she'd assumed the women were just running late.

Liam grabbed his cell phone and quickly dialed Emma's number. It rang five times before going to voice mail. He hung up and dialed again, with the same results. He told Jane to call her from Morning Glory's number to see if she would answer if she thought it was work.

It rang and rang, but Emma didn't answer. They both knew something was very wrong. Jane began crying and apologizing for keeping Emma's plans a secret. Liam reminded her that she was Emma's friend and was simply doing what she was asked. They both tried Morgan's cell phone as well, but didn't get an answer.

They locked up the coffee shop and went next door together. Jane called Sadie and told her something was wrong, and to meet them at Emma's house. They'd need all their resources to figure out what was going on.

Liam's mind played out a hundred different scenarios. He worried that she may have gone into preterm labor. His instincts told him she was in danger, but he had no idea why. She wasn't running late, and she hadn't lost track of time. He could feel that something was very wrong.

He'd felt "off" all day, and he could kick himself for not figuring it out sooner. If he had, Emma would be home.

He was doing his wife no good by dwelling on what might have been, so he decided it was better to take action. He tried calling again, but there was still no answer.

About that time, Colin came downstairs with a solemn

look on his face. He looked sick as he handed Liam a piece of paper. "Liam, I found somethin'. 'Tis bad."

Liam studied the document as an array of emotions played across his face. He looked desperately at Colin, but the man simply nodded to let Liam know there was no mistaking what he read.

"This can't be true. How did I miss this?" Liam dropped the paper on the counter and collapsed onto the bar stool, his head in his hands.

Sadie picked up the paper and gasped as she read its contents. It was a copy of the visitors' log at the Ohio State Penitentiary.

"When you told me what happened to Emma before, I had a hunch that all of the strange happenings were linked to Xavier and his cronies. I called the prison and they faxed me the document," Colin explained.

The paper listed every visitor who had met with Xavier since his incarceration. Jane peered over Sadie's shoulder for a better view, and her eyes filled with fresh tears as she read the list.

Xavier Smith had one faithful visitor. Every Sunday for the past several months, the same name was logged.

With a voice that sent panic through the group and caused Liam's blood to run cold, Sadie read out the name that appeared over and over.

"Morgan Turner."

THIRTY-ONE

EMMA OPENED HER EYES AS THE MORNING LIGHT FILTERED through the cracked window panes. The sun was up, and she was grateful for the tiny bit of warmth it provided.

She was freezing. Her body trembled and her teeth chattered. She'd spent the night curled in the fetal position on the filthy mattress, relying solely on her own body heat for warmth. It had been a restless night. The rope cut into her neck each time she shifted; if she moved too far, it choked her. Every inch of her heavily pregnant body hurt. She felt as if she would never be warm again.

She scanned the room and noticed she was alone. She had no idea where Morgan was, but she had no doubt her captor would return soon. Until that moment, she hadn't left Emma's side for a second. She'd played "Goodnight, Sweetheart" over and over all night long on the record player. Emma knew Morgan was trying to drive her insane, and truth be told, she wasn't far off.

Throughout the seemingly endless night, Morgan tortured Emma with stories of what she would do to her children if she tried to escape. Emma didn't doubt her words.

Morgan said she would kill Liam, and she reminded Emma that she'd already tried when she cut his brake lines. She said the next time she would be successful.

Around dawn, Emma passed out from exhaustion. Morgan had been unmoved by Emma's pleas for mercy. The insanity in her eyes convinced Emma that her captor was barely human. She had no soul, and no compassion; she would kill Emma if it served her purpose, whatever that may be. Emma berated herself for being stupid enough to believe the woman was her friend.

Emma had no idea if she was more valuable to Morgan dead or alive. She blamed Emma for alienating Xavier's affections, and as much as she tried to convince Morgan that she had no interest in the psychopath, it didn't matter. Emma wasn't sure if Morgan thought she was lying, or if her feelings were simply inconsequential. All that seemed to matter was that Xavier was supposedly in love with Emma. Therefore, her life must be destroyed.

Morgan was unstable, and Emma had no experience dealing with mental issues. She wished for the thousandth time that Liam was there. He must be out of his mind with worry, and it broke her heart that she was the one to blame for ending up here. Everyone had warned her about Morgan, and she was blind. She'd believed Morgan was a good person on the inside.

Emma slowly rolled over and maneuvered her body until she was resting on her knees. Light-headed from the drugs, as well as from hunger and dehydration, she took a breath and pushed herself to a standing position. The rope was barely long enough for Emma to stand to her full height. She was careful not to stretch it to the limit. Peering out the window, she saw no sign of Morgan. Craning her neck as far as she could, she saw smoke coming from the car's exhaust.

Morgan was sitting inside, talking on her phone. She'd

taken Emma's purse and thrown it in the trunk before leading her into the cabin. Her phone was in her purse, and even if she had it, the battery would be dead.

Looking around, Emma hoped to find something sharp to cut the rope, but there was nothing. The room had been cleared of all its contents, and besides, the rope wasn't long enough to leave the mattress.

True desperation set in. Until that moment, she'd held out hope that the situation wasn't as dire as it appeared. In that instant, Emma believed she could very well die there. She and her baby were in grave danger, and there was nothing she could do.

She sank to her knees and began to cry. She missed Liam and her daughters so much that it physically hurt. Her crying turned to sobbing, her body shaking with each gut-wrenching breath.

Suddenly, Emma screamed as her abdomen was gripped with a pain so intense it took her breath away. It was followed quickly by another pain, equally as severe. Emma was having contractions. They were not the Braxton-Hicks pains she'd experienced earlier in her pregnancy—they were genuine, labor-inducing contractions. Her baby was going to be born in that shack, right there on the stained mattress.

She screamed again. No one came, not even Morgan.

After a few minutes, the pains subsided. Emma prayed that real labor hadn't started. Her baby could not be born there. She willed herself to calm down and breathe deeply. She closed her eyes and pretended she was home with her family. After several minutes, the pains didn't return.

Emma might not have been in active labor, but it wouldn't be long before she was. She had to find a way out.

Seventy-two hours after Emma's disappearance, Liam had his team of reinforcements in place. Several Beckland police officers and many of Liam's fellow FBI agents had taken over the O'Reilly house. The kitchen served as their makeshift headquarters, each person responsible for a distinct job.

Sadie and Jane worked diligently, covering the town with "Missing" posters of Emma. Morning Glory remained closed, and Jane and Sadie tried to keep the days as normal as possible for the girls, which was easier said than done. The children spent most of their days in tears, asking when their mama was coming home.

Liam hadn't slept a wink since Emma disappeared. He was exhausted, but determined that he wouldn't rest until his wife was home. He caffeinated himself with a steady stream of coffee, but the dark circles under his eyes and haggard look on his face told the truth. He was using every institution at his disposal, and calling in every favor he'd ever been owed.

He'd never been so terrified in his life. Emma was out

there somewhere, and he had to find her. The fact that she was pregnant made her even more vulnerable, and he continued to play out every horrible scenario he could envision. Each one ended worse than the last. Morgan's and Emma's faces were plastered all over every newspaper throughout the entire state, and the story was on all the TV news channels. If the women were anywhere near people, someone was bound to recognize them.

Reporters surrounded the house, waiting like vultures for scraps of news. Normally that type of invasion would anger him, but Liam wanted Emma's story on as many venues as possible. A tip line was set up, and a steady stream of calls had been pouring in since the previous night. Most of them weren't helpful, but one woman called in and said she'd seen a car matching the description of Morgan's at a roadside diner on the way to Warfield. Armed with this new information, the team widened the search parameters, but there was still no sign of Emma or Morgan.

Liam knew someone who might have the answers he needed, so he was on his way to the Ohio State Penitentiary. As much as he couldn't stand the thought of sharing the same air as Xavier Smith, he had no choice. Once he'd understood that Morgan had a connection to Xavier, he knew he had to talk to the man. Xavier might be Emma's best chance at survival.

Liam parked his car and entered the dreary prison building. After making his way through security, he followed the guard down the bleak hallway and into the private meeting room he'd requested. After waiting a few minutes, Xavier sauntered into the room.

Rather than deteriorating in prison, Xavier appeared robust and healthy. He'd been taking advantage of the prison weight room, and his large frame boasted chiseled muscles, defined through the orange prison jumpsuit. Liam's blood boiled as he looked at the monster who had tortured and beaten Emma. If he hadn't needed Xavier so much, Liam would have gladly ripped him to pieces with his bare hands.

"What happened to her? She's all over the news." Xavier spoke through clenched teeth as Liam sat across the table from him.

"How dare you question me. You're responsible for this. She's missing, just like you and that psycho girlfriend of yours planned." Liam tried to keep his emotions in check. He reminded himself that he needed the information Xavier had in order to save Emma's life.

"I didn't plan this. I didn't even know she was gone. This is your fault." Xavier pounded his fists angrily on the table.

"Listen here, you monster. My wife is missing, and your girlfriend is responsible. You're gonna sit there and tell me you didn't know about it?" Anger shot from Liam's eyes like arrows plunging toward a target.

"You can either believe me or not, O'Reilly, but I would never hurt Emma. I love her," Xavier hissed.

"Love her? You broke into her house and beat her within an inch of her life!" Liam's anger was unleashed, and he didn't know if he could get it under control.

"I did what I had to do. But yes, I do love her. We belong together. That's probably what set Morgan off, now that I think about it." Xavier looked as if a lightbulb had gone off inside his head.

"If you know something, you'd better tell me now!"

Liam's voice reverberated loudly as he threw the keys he'd been clenching across the room. They hit the wall and bounced onto the floor with a pinging sound. He jumped up, knocking the metal chair over in the process. He needed to get a handle on himself, so he turned his back to Xavier and raked his hands through his hair in frustration.

"Morgan is in love with me. I may have led her to believe

that the feeling was mutual. It became hard for me to conceal my feelings for Emma, and Morgan figured it out. I needed her help, so I strung her along. It was all in the name of true love." Xavier spoke quietly, but the words were deafening in the silent room.

Liam looked at the man sitting in front of him. Xavier's steel-gray eyes had taken on a faraway look, and Liam could literally see his touch with reality slipping away. He had to act fast if he was going to get answers.

"Where was Morgan supposed to take Emma when she kidnapped her for you, Xavier? You said you needed her help. What did you ask her to do?"

Liam leaned forward and placed his hands on the table, close to Xavier, coaxing gently, hoping to draw him out.

"You've got it all wrong. She wasn't supposed to do anything to Emma. You were her target, O'Reilly. Her job was to turn your head away from your wife. She was supposed to be a distraction for you. She's a beautiful woman, don't you agree?" Xavier looked slyly into Liam's eyes.

"Your plan went very wrong, Xavier," Liam replied.

"Apparently she was too stupid to make it work. She must have taken matters into her own hands. I should have known she was up to something from the way she acted last week. I accidentally said I was in love with Emma, and she snapped. She said I was going to be sorry. I swear, if she hurts Emma, I will kill her myself!" Xavier pounded his large fists on the table again, gaining the attention of the guard standing outside of the door.

"Listen to me, Xavier." Liam leaned farther across the table and grabbed the front of Xavier's prison shirt. "If you have any idea what she may have done with Emma, you tell me." Liam tried to control the desperation in his voice, but it was no use. "You say you love her. If that's true, you might be the only one who can save her."

"I foresee a deal in my future." Xavier's smile was cold and chilling. "I have an address. It's a cozy little place that I'd planned to take Emma once I found a way out of this joint. You might want to check there." His voice turned menacing. "Morgan has gone off the deep end. There's no telling what she'll do. You should have taken better care of your wife."

Xavier rattled off the address, and Liam put it into his phone's GPS. Without wasting another second, he ran back to the parking lot. The location was three hours away.

He grabbed his phone, dialed quickly, and gave the address to Colin and the other FBI agents, who said they were on their way. Praying he wasn't too late, Liam punched the gas pedal to the floor and sped down the highway.

THIRTY-THREE

Emma had no idea how many days she'd been there. She'd stopped keeping track. Hopelessness had taken over, and she felt as if she'd been swallowed up in a black hole. She'd stopped having contractions, but now she had a new concern.

Daisy's movements had grown sporadic, and Emma was consumed with the fear that something was very wrong with her baby. Morgan had fed her nothing but crackers and water. Emma was weak, hungry, exhausted, and dizzy. She had to escape before Morgan killed both her and the baby, but she didn't know how.

Emma had begun hallucinating, drifting in and out of consciousness, never sure what was real and what was in her mind. She'd dreamed of her mother again, drifting back to the safe haven of her childhood.

She was lying across her mother's lap as she stroked Emma's strawberry-blonde curls and told her how much she loved her. She whispered in Emma's ear that she was strong. Emma was a child in the dream, and she giggled, telling her mother that her daddy was strong. Emma's mom looked her in the eye.

"Emma, you are stronger than you know. Someday you will have to pull that strength from somewhere deep inside of you."

In Emma's little-girl mind, that made no sense, but she nodded anyway.

The dream took her from past to present, and her mama was there, once again, telling the adult version of Emma to find her strength.

Emma didn't know if she was remembering an actual event, or if she was dreaming of something that had never happened. When she woke, her face was drenched in tears.

The dreams were telling her that she must summon the strength from within to fight back, but she didn't know if she could. In her weakened state, she wasn't strong enough to overpower Morgan physically, and with a rope tied around her neck, she couldn't run.

Frustration mixed with fear, and despair played on her mind, telling her she was going to die there. Emma thought of her girls and Liam. She imagined how terrified they must be. She racked her brain to come up with a plan, but nothing revealed itself.

Morgan had barely spoken, so Emma had no idea what the endgame would be. She tried to ask questions, but Morgan refused to answer. The only thing she said was that Emma was getting exactly what she deserved. Her worst fear was that Morgan was keeping her alive long enough to give birth and would then steal the baby. Even if she couldn't save herself, she had to find a way to save Daisy.

Emma worked up the courage to plead with her again. Morgan ignored the supplication, so Emma pushed a little harder. She knew immediately that she'd gone too far. Morgan punched Emma as hard as she could and her head snapped back, causing the rope to cut into her neck even more. Morgan grabbed Emma's hair and punched her yet again. The force knocked Emma from her kneeling position, and she fell back onto the mattress. Morgan looked at her with disgust, turned on her heels, and walked out the front door.

Emma was sobbing and bleeding, and she didn't know how much longer she could hold on. She was angry that something so horrible was happening to her once again. She'd been in a hostage situation twice within the same year. Things like that didn't happen to people like Emma. She was just a normal woman, a mom, who only wanted to live out her life with her husband and daughters.

Anger and frustration boiled inside of her, bubbling like a volcano on the verge of eruption. She screamed loudly. No one answered.

Emma rolled from her back to her side, crying so hard that her body shook. A sharp object poked into her hip, and she thought there must be something hard sticking out of the mattress. She moved, and as she did, she saw it. Lying on the filthy mattress was Liam's pocketknife. She'd slid it into the back pocket of her maternity jeans after finding it in the laundry room, planning to give it to him. She'd been so preoccupied with escaping for a day of fun that she'd totally forgotten about it.

Emma wiped her tears, knowing her miracle had come. There was a light at the end of the tunnel, and it was shining brightly. All she had to do was cut the rope around her neck and make a break for it. But she had to plan her strategy carefully, because she'd only get one shot to do it right. If she made a mistake, the golden opportunity would slip right through her hands.

THIRTY-FOUR

Liam sped down the freeway, trying to outrun the fear that followed closely behind him. Emma had been gone more than three days, and he was terrified for her safety, not to mention the safety of his unborn daughter. He kept telling himself that he would find them. He had an address, and unless Xavier had sent him on a wild-goose chase, he should arrive at the cabin in little more than an hour.

It was torturous, knowing Emma was in danger and he couldn't stop it. In his years as an FBI agent, Liam had seen more than a few hostage situations gone wrong. He would never forgive himself if something happened to his wife. She and the girls were his entire world. He was a fixer, and it killed him that he hadn't been able to fix the situation. He tried not to think of the atrocities that Emma may have endured, focusing instead on what was ahead. He needed to be calm and steady, prepared for anything.

Emma was strong, and she would fight to the bitter end to protect their child. He was counting on it.

Liam floored the accelerator and watched the speedometer climb.

"Hold on, Emma. I'm coming."

THIRTY-FIVE

Morgan had been outside for a while, and Emma knew she had to work fast for her plan to be successful. With trembling hands, she opened the pocketknife, wishing the tiny blade were larger. It was the equivalent of bringing a stick to a gun fight, but it was all she had.

The rope around her neck was thick, so it would be a tedious process. She raised the blade to the rope and began quick, back-and-forth sawing motions, making sure she didn't prick her chin as she worked. The small threads of the rope began to unravel, but she wasn't even close to breaking through. Her hands trembled as she sawed frantically, keeping close watch out the window of the front door. After only a couple of minutes, her arms began cramping. Emma's energy stores were depleted; even the smallest amount of exertion was exhausting.

Lowering her hands, she gave them a few quick shakes, flexing her fingers and wrists in an attempt to revive them. Time was running out, so she began the grueling process again. Her arms screamed for mercy, but she didn't relent, pushing through the pain. She was making progress, and the fibers of the rope grew thinner.

She pushed on, tears coursing down her face as she felt the thick rope around her neck give way. Grabbing it with both hands, she pulled the ends apart and felt blissful freedom. She clicked the knife shut and stuffed it back into her pocket.

Morgan approached the front door, so Emma wrapped the ends of the rope back around her neck and curled up on the mattress facing the wall. If Emma's back was toward the front door, Morgan would think she was sleeping. She willed her body to remain still and rehearsed her escape plan.

Her captor always came inside at night to sleep. Morgan had a far more comfortable sleeping arrangement than Emma, with an air mattress, warm blankets, and pillows. In contrast, Emma shivered and froze all night long and struggled to find the smallest comfort. It didn't matter. Emma was determined that her nights in captivity were over. Once Morgan went to sleep, she would make a break for it.

As the darkness settled over the cabin like a thick blanket, Morgan climbed into bed, ready to sleep. Emma had noticed that the other woman was a heavy sleeper, so she didn't anticipate any problems. Emma was too weak for a fight, so the only solution was to sneak out while she slept.

Emma waited to hear the sounds of Morgan's steady breathing, letting her know it was time to propel the plan into action. Her heart raced, and she prayed she'd be strong enough to carry out the mission. She had one shot to do it right. Emma's gut told her there would be no second chance if she failed. Either she escaped, or she'd die here.

Emma thought of Liam and her daughters. She had to get back to them. They needed her. She pictured each of their dear faces, knowing that when the moment came, she'd draw her strength from them.

After what seemed like an eternity, Morgan's steady, even breathing indicated she was sleeping. Emma pushed herself to a sitting position and removed the rope from her neck. Using the wall for support, she managed to stand. She was wobbly and weak from lack of movement, but determination grew inside of her. Taking several deep breaths, Emma gingerly began her hundred-mile journey toward the door. She moved slowly, trying to silence the creaking of the old floorboards beneath her feet. They groaned as she stepped on them. She crept at a snail's pace, moving toward her target.

Emma reached out in the darkness, grasping the rusty doorknob and breathing a sigh of relief that she'd made it. With trepidation, she turned the ancient knob, her pulse quickening and her stomach lurching at the squeaking sound it made in the silence.

Morgan sat up quickly, shining her flashlight into the darkness. Looking toward the mattress in the corner, she gasped as she realized Emma wasn't there. Her eyes darted to the front door and she sprang from her bed, the situation registering in her brain immediately.

It was the moment of truth. Emma's adrenaline kicked in and told her it was time to fight. Shoving her hand into her pocket, Emma grabbed the pocketknife and flicked it open. Holding the doorframe with one hand for support, she brandished the weapon as if it were a sword. Morgan sprinted across the floor toward her.

Emma had one chance. She held her arm out straight and plunged the knife deeply into Morgan's stomach, giving it an extra push as it dug into flesh. The shock of the thrust registered on Morgan's face, and the woman's blue eyes opened wide in surprise. Morgan's flashlight clattered onto the floor as she doubled over and dropped to her knees, clutching her stomach while she screamed.

Without a second's hesitation, Emma waddled as fast as she could out the front door, spotting Morgan's car. Looking behind her, Emma saw Morgan slumped on the floor, half inside and half outside of the cabin.

Opening the driver side door, Emma prayed she'd find the keys in the ignition. Miraculously, they were there. She jumped inside and turned on the starter. Jamming the vehicle into Reverse, Emma did a three-point turn and screeched down the lane as fast as she could. She had no clue where she was going, but she knew she was free.

THIRTY-SIX

LIAM ARRIVED AT THE RUN-DOWN SHACK, GRATEFUL OTHER detectives and policemen were already there. He slammed the car into Park, jumped out and sprinted toward the house. He couldn't wait to wrap Emma in his arms and never let her go.

Approaching the cabin, he was met by a grave-faced detective. Liam knew something was wrong.

The detective cut straight to the chase. "She's not here."

"What do you mean, she's not here? Xavier said this was where Morgan would go." Liam's heart beat nervously in his chest.

"Morgan's here, but Emma isn't. She was, though, and it was bad. It looks like your wife was held under rough circumstances. You may not want to see it." The detective placed his hand on Liam's shoulder, partially for comfort, but also to discourage him from going inside the shack.

"If Emma was here, I need to see it. I have to know everything."

Liam pushed past the detective and took the sagging porch steps two at a time. Entering the cabin, he first noticed the sparseness of the situation. There was nothing in the room except for what must have been Morgan's sleeping area, and a filthy mattress. Liam's stomach clenched as he surveyed Emma's prison. Bile rose in his stomach and he pushed down the need to vomit. His pregnant wife had been forced to lie on that horrible mattress without even the comfort of a single blanket or pillow. It was freezing; wherever she was, Emma must be nearly hypothermic.

The most disturbing aspect was the rope that was tied to a spike driven into the floorboards next to the mattress. Crossing the room and crouching down, he picked up the rope. His heart leaped in his chest when he saw it had been sawed in half.

Piecing together the situation in his mind, he concluded that Emma had found some type of implement to saw through the rope, probably the same object she used to stab Morgan when she made her escape. He assumed Morgan's car had brought them there, but it was nowhere to be found. Maybe Emma had used it to run.

He had no idea where she was, or if she was even alive, but he refused to listen to the dark thoughts in his mind. He needed to think she was fine. He instructed the police officers to put out an APB on Morgan's car. If Emma was out there, he was going to find her.

THIRTY-SEVEN

Emma sped down the unfamiliar dirt road, crying so hysterically that she could barely see in front of her. She tried to calm down, but she was terrified. She didn't know where she was, and she had no idea where she was going. She continued driving, hoping she'd see signs of civilization, but there was nothing but trees on all sides. There were no road signs, and she started to wonder if she was driving in circles.

She pulled to the side of the road and put the car into Park. Glancing at the dashboard, Emma realized Morgan's car was on empty. She turned off the engine to conserve fuel while she worked on a plan. Fumbling for the dome light, Emma saw Morgan's cell phone lying on the passenger seat. All she had to do was call Liam and he would find her.

Grabbing the phone, her hopes were dashed. There was no service. She dialed Liam's number anyway, praying that by some miracle the call would go through. It didn't. She tried sending a text, but that failed as well.

All she could think to do was drive until she came into an area with phone reception. She had to reach one eventually.

But when she turned the key in the ignition, nothing happened.

She moved it to the Off position and tried again. The engine didn't even turn over. She desperately tried two more times, but the car wouldn't start. Emma knew she must keep moving. Morgan may have followed her. Emma had no idea how badly wounded she was, and she wasn't about to take a chance on sitting still. She decided to continue on foot.

The temperature was steadily dropping, and small snowflakes began to fall. Emma wasn't dressed appropriately for winter weather in her jeans and blouse, but she refused to give up. She rummaged through the car for a coat, but there was nothing. She opened the trunk and found her purse and dead cell phone. She also saw a wool blanket and decided that was better than nothing.

The night was so cold that she could see her breath. She grabbed the blanket, wrapped it tightly around her shoulders, and began walking, telling herself that she had to keep taking one step after another. Her feet were completely numb, but she refused to entertain the idea that she probably had frostbite. All that mattered was finding help.

Emma's teeth chattered and her body shook, but she trudged on. Snowflakes collected on her eyelashes, and she blinked them away. The adrenaline she'd experienced at the cabin had begun to wear off. The only thing left was exhaustion. She was starving, and her throat was so parched that it felt like sandpaper. Daisy hadn't moved in hours, and Emma was terrified that something was wrong. She kept moving, but at her slow pace, she knew finding help would take an eternity.

It was pitch black, and the moon was only a sliver in the inky sky. In the distance, coyotes howled. Emma was frightened of what might be lurking in the darkness. There could be bears and wolves. She didn't want to find out. Instead, she forced her brain to replay every happy memory she could think of in an attempt to keep herself motivated. She envisioned Liam and her precious daughters, reminding herself that she had to get home to them.

She'd been walking for what seemed like hours when she began to feel dizzy. Her legs felt as if they were mired in quicksand. Every step required superhuman effort, and she had none left.

The trees began to spin, and the ground came up to meet Emma as her body gave in to the exhaustion she could no longer fight. Her head hit the dirt road and she whispered Liam's name into the cold night air.

THIRTY-EIGHT

LIAM DROVE AROUND FOR TWO HOURS ON THE ABANDONED dirt roads surrounding the cabin. The other detectives were still at the crime scene, looking for more clues and finishing the investigation. The medical examiner had arrived, and Morgan's lifeless body had been transported to the morgue. Emma's thrusting stab had found its mark, and Morgan had bled out by the time the police arrived.

Liam wasn't sorry that Morgan was dead, but he wished she'd stayed alive long enough to be interrogated. There were many questions that might never be answered, most importantly Emma's whereabouts and physical state. Liam could only imagine what his wife had been through. Time was running out for the outcome to be favorable.

It didn't matter. Liam would not stop searching. He scoured each and every bend of the back roads, praying while he drove. Emma would be fine. He refused to believe anything else.

THIRTY-NINE

Leon and Mavis Masters drove in companionable silence down the old dirt road toward their home. Normally they wouldn't be returning from town at such a late hour, but Leon wanted an apple pie, so they'd made the ten-mile drive into Smithville. The older couple adhered to a pretty predictable schedule, but every so often they did something spontaneous. It had been one of those days.

They'd done their shopping and had supper at their favorite diner in town. It had been quite a treat. Leon ordered the chicken pot pie, and Mavis had the roast beef. For the most part, they liked eating at home, but on certain occasions it was nice for someone else to do the cooking.

The meal had been mostly enjoyable, except for the news bulletin about that poor missing woman from Beckland. The story was on every television station, and Mavis's heart went out to the young mother. The world just wasn't a safe place anymore. Hopefully the woman would be found and returned safely to her family.

Leon hummed to himself while Mavis stared out the front window, watching the snowflakes fall quietly to the ground. The snow started while they were in town, and Mavis was glad they'd be home soon. She wanted to get there before too much snow accumulated.

Mavis was lost in thought, thinking about baking her apple pie. Suddenly she saw something in the middle of the road.

"Leon, stop! Look! Something is up there!" Mavis reached across the seat and laid her hand on her husband's arm to get his attention.

"Well I'll be. You're right. Wonder what it is." Leon brought the truck to a stop as his headlights illuminated the heap in the road. "You stay here, Mavis. I'll take a look. Maybe it's a deer."

Mavis watched as Leon crossed in front of the truck and crouched down to inspect it. He yelled something, but Mavis couldn't hear it from inside the truck. She opened the door.

"It's a woman, and she's frozen almost to death! Mavis, help me get her up."

Leon tried to move the woman, but Mavis knew he couldn't do it alone. He might be strong for seventy-five years old, but he'd need help in order to maneuver a person.

"Oh my goodness! She's unconscious, Leon. We have to get her into town. The police will know what to do to help her."

Together, Mavis and Leon pulled the heavily pregnant stranger to her feet. The woman's eyes flew open, and Mavis could see that she was terrified.

"Darlin', it's okay. You're safe now. Let's get you inside the truck. We'll get you some help."

Leon and Mavis propped the woman between them and slowly walked her to the vehicle. They moved her into the back seat of the truck. As the dome light shone on the stranger's face, Mavis caught her breath. It was the same woman she'd just seen on the news. She was the missing mother everyone was looking for. Mavis couldn't believe they'd found her.

They covered her with the large blanket they kept in the truck. Mavis instructed Leon to crank up the heat and he obliged. She wedged herself into the back seat with the woman and tried to help her drink some water. The poor woman coughed and sputtered as the liquid went into her mouth, and Mavis wondered how long she had been without sustenance. She feared for the child the woman was carrying. The outcome for the baby might not be good.

The woman hadn't said a word since they found her. She simply sat there sobbing. Mavis could only imagine what the poor thing had endured, and she scooted a little closer to the stranger and put her arm around her. Maybe she'd take some comfort from human contact.

"You're going to be okay now, dear. We're going to get you into Smithville. There's no hospital there, but the police will know what to do."

Mavis wished she could remember what the news reporter said the missing woman's name was, but for the life of her, she couldn't. All she could do was try to comfort the poor woman as Leon sped into town.

FORTY

Thirty-five minutes later, they arrived in Smithville. Leon angled the truck straight for the police station. He raced into the parking lot and found a space. Slamming it into Park, he went inside. A couple of minutes later, Leon and Sheriff Rogers trotted back outside and opened the back door. The woman jumped when she saw the sheriff, but he spoke to her soothingly, assuring her that he was there to help. Between the two men, they got her into the police station.

Sheriff Rogers knew she was the missing woman on all the news reports, so he called the tip line that was scrolling across the television screen in the police station holding room. Mavis and Leon sat on either side of the woman. The sheriff told them her name was Emma O'Reilly. She still hadn't said a word, just stared off into the distance as tears rolled down her face. Mavis knew she was in shock, so she didn't push her to talk.

They sat there for thirty minutes while Sheriff Rogers made phone calls to find out what they should do. Suddenly Emma doubled over and screamed. A stream of liquid gushed onto the police station floor. The men had no idea what was happening, but Mavis knew Emma's water had broken, signaling the start of labor. Time was running out. Emma needed to get to a hospital as soon as possible.

"Sheriff Rogers, Emma needs a doctor, and she needs one now. You need to call the ambulance from Warfield and tell them to get here." Mavis had five children of her own, and she knew the signs of labor. In Emma's weakened state, she might have a traumatic childbirth ahead of her.

Unfortunately, Smithville was forty minutes away from Warfield. The ambulance wouldn't arrive for some time. Mavis had attended the births of all her neighbors' children and was a fairly decent stand-in midwife. Even though she wasn't equipped for what would probably be a high-risk delivery, she was grateful for a few skills that might come in handy.

Emma was in a full-blown state of panic. She screamed and cried out in pain, on the verge of hysteria. She was in turmoil, but she had to get her panic under control if there was any chance for a happy outcome.

"Emma, look at me." Mavis held Emma's face in her hands and forced the woman to lock eyes with her. "I know you're scared, and I know you're in pain. Your baby is ready to be born, though, honey, and I need your help. Focus on my face. Don't think of anything else."

Mavis watched as Emma slowly came back to reality. Understanding dawned in the woman's eyes.

Emma nodded as she realized she was close to giving birth. "I'm scared. My baby hasn't moved for a long time." Her voice trembled.

"Honey, you must be one strong woman to have made it this far. We're going to push those bad thoughts away and think of good things. What's your baby's name?"

"Daisy. Her name is Daisy." Emma smiled for the first time.

"That's a beautiful name. Do you have other children?" Mavis already knew the answer from the news coverage, but she wanted Emma to focus on those girls and forget her fear.

"I have three girls: Lily, Rose, and Dahlia. I miss them so mu—" Emma let out a scream as another pain gripped her weary body.

"Look at me, Emma!" Mavis tried to distract her from the pain. "Your girls are going to be so happy to meet their baby sister."

"Liam... I want Liam," Emma murmured as her eyes drifted closed. She was about to lose consciousness.

"Emma, open your eyes. Tell me about Liam."

"My husband... I need him!" Emma's eyes flew open as she screamed in pain.

Mavis had to motivate the woman to hold on. She ran to the desk and told the sheriff to bring the phone to her, then asked Emma if she could remember Liam's phone number. Emma nodded, reciting the numbers as Mavis dialed. The phone rang three times. Mavis prayed someone would answer.

"O'Reilly," said the man on the other end.

"Liam, my name is Mavis, and I'm with your wife. We found her on the road, and we're at the police station in Smithville waiting for an ambulance. Emma is in labor. She needs to hear your voice."

Mavis breathed a sigh of relief as she held the phone up to Emma's ear.

FORTY-ONE

THE PAIN WAS SO INTENSE THAT EMMA COULD BARELY concentrate, but when Mavis placed the phone to her ear and Liam's voice was on the other end, she snapped to attention.

"Emma! Emma, can you hear me?" There was panic in her husband's voice.

"Liam—" There was so much Emma wanted to say, but her body was gripped by another contraction and she screamed.

Mavis took the phone, and Emma heard her tell Liam that she was being taken to Warfield Regional Hospital. All she could think of at that moment was the pain. Her body was being ripped in half and she was simply along for the ride. All that mattered was making it through the next contraction.

Emma tried to remember her Lamaze breathing, but she was so weak that her brain wasn't functioning. The pain was intense. Something had to be wrong with Daisy. Everything felt different than she remembered from her other births. Emma gritted her teeth and prayed the contraction would end. She drifted in and out of consciousness. She tried to focus on Mavis's worried face, but her body wouldn't cooperate.

Mavis said the ambulance had arrived. Emma focused on keeping her eyes open, but another pain gripped her body and she squeezed them shut. Mavis commanded Emma to look at her, so she opened her eyes again. The room began to spin. Mavis's face moved farther away, just a small speck in the distance. Giving in to the darkness, Emma closed her eyes once more.

When she woke, she had no clue where she was. There was an oxygen mask on her face. The motion around her told her she must be in the ambulance. Her contractions weren't as strong. Emma assumed the worst.

"My baby…."

Emma looked frantically at the paramedic kneeling beside her. Her voice sounded muffled and strange inside the oxygen mask.

"Mrs. O'Reilly, I need you to relax. You're in active labor, and you're already dilated to five centimeters. At the rate you're progressing, we may not make it to the hospital in time. You have an IV, so you're getting fluids. You're severely dehydrated and malnourished. Labor is going to be difficult. I gave you some Demerol to take the edge off the contractions, but if you were hoping for an epidural, you're out of luck." The paramedic smiled kindly.

"Is my baby okay?" Emma was afraid of the answer, but she had to know.

"We don't have fetal monitors in the ambulance." The man didn't answer the question, and his evasion did little to calm her fears.

"How much longer… until… we're at the hospital?" Emma breathed through the contraction that had started.

"Not long now, Mrs. O'Reilly. We're about five minutes away."

Emma tried to steady her breath as the contraction released. She panted, knowing another would begin soon. She was relieved that they were almost at the hospital and hoped Liam would be there waiting. She needed his strength to get through it.

The ambulance lurched to a stop and the back doors flew open. The warmth of the vehicle was invaded by the biting cold night air, and goose bumps erupted on Emma's flesh. The paramedic covered her with a warm blanket, and it blocked a bit of the chill as her body was lowered from the ambulance. The wheels met the pavement, and she was whisked into the emergency room at top speed. Liam was nowhere to be found.

A man met her at the door and introduced himself as Dr. Nelson. The light panels on the ceiling raced before her eyes. Another contraction began and she panted, telling herself that she wasn't going to scream. She needed to conserve what little energy she had left.

They rolled her into a room, and two nurses helped transport her from the gurney onto a birthing bed. In between the contractions that were growing stronger by the minute, the nurses helped her out of her filthy clothes and into a hospital gown. Even with the filter of the Demerol, the contractions were growing in intensity and coming much more frequently. Emma closed her eyes tightly and concentrated on not screaming. What she really wanted to do was open her mouth and wail.

Dr. Nelson said she needed to be examined, and she felt pressure as he began. The contractions were coming hard and fast, with little time in between. From experience, Emma knew things were moving quickly. She prayed Liam would arrive in time.

"Mrs. O'Reilly, you're dilated to ten and fully effaced. You're hooked up to the fetal monitor, and your baby's heartbeat is more sluggish than I would like. I've been briefed on your ordeal, and I'm concerned for your baby's well-being. We need to get this baby delivered. I want you to go ahead and push." Dr. Nelson went to the sink and scrubbed his hands in preparation.

"But… Liam. Where is Liam?" Emma was frantic. She needed her husband if she was going to be able to get through it.

"I know you want your husband, honey, but your baby isn't going to wait." The nurse smoothed Emma's hair and smiled kindly. It did little to soothe her.

Emma's abdomen was squeezed once again as a contraction began, but she also felt the familiar pressure letting her know Daisy was anxious to make her entrance into the world. Emma gritted her teeth and let out a yell, unable to control it. Tears streamed down her face, partially from the pain, but mostly from the fact that Liam wasn't there. He was going to miss the birth of his daughter.

Anger surged inside of her. Of all the things Morgan had done, stealing a precious moment away from them was the worst. If it weren't for Morgan, Liam would be there.

FORTY-TWO

There was a crash as someone burst through the door, knocking over a rolling table in the process. Emma was so engrossed in bearing down to push that she didn't even look toward the sound.

"Emma!"

Her head snapped up as she heard Liam's voice.

"Liam, you're here!" She sobbed as her husband reached her side.

"You didn't think I'd miss this, did you?" Tears streamed down his face as he smiled.

"I… didn't think—" She tried to finish the thought, but a scream came out instead as her body was ripped in half. There were so many things she wanted to say, but they would have to wait. She had to push.

Liam held her hand, supporting her as he sat on the bed. She braced her back against his strong body. Emma pushed again, and Dr. Nelson said the baby was crowning. She was almost there.

Taking a deep breath, Emma bore down, digging deeply into every reservoir of strength she possessed. She pushed with all her might, but she was so tired. Her fortitude was wearing thin.

"I can't… it hurts so much," she cried.

"Yes you can. You're the strongest woman I've ever known. Look at what you've been through, and here you are, still going. I love you so much."

Liam stood and placed his face in front of Emma's so all she could see was his eyes. She remembered the first time she'd seen him, that day in her coffee shop. She'd been lost in his eyes ever since. He reminded her just how tough she was.

"One more push, Emma. That's all I need. Just one more." Dr. Nelson's words of encouragement were the impetus she needed.

She locked her eyes on Liam's, almost hypnotically. She took a deep breath and funneled every last ounce of power she had inside, gripping Liam's hands as she pushed. There was one last strain of pressure, then a release. Daisy was out.

Exhaustion tried to take over, but she willed herself to stay awake. She had to hear her baby cry. She had to know the baby was healthy before she could collapse. She listened, but all she heard was silence.

"Why isn't she crying?" Emma tried to push herself to a sitting position, but she was too weak. "Liam?"

Liam gripped his wife's hand as he stood riveted in place. Fear covered his face. Dr. Nelson and the nurses were bent over the baby, moving quickly and speaking in hushed voices. Emma's heart beat rapidly. She prayed harder than she ever had in her life. Daisy had to be all right, after everything they'd been through.

Suddenly the deafening silence in the room was interrupted by the sweet sounds of a baby's cry. Emma was certain that it was the most beautiful sound she'd ever heard. Dr. Nelson placed Daisy into her mother's waiting arms.

With trembling hands, Emma cradled the precious bundle close to her heart.

"Is she all right?" Emma asked hopefully.

"This little girl is a fighter, just like her mama. She's perfect, and considering what the two of you have been through, that's nothing short of a miracle." Dr. Nelson smiled broadly.

"Thank you," Emma whispered.

"We'll give you some time alone," the nurse said as she and Dr. Nelson left the room.

Emma handed Daisy to Liam and watched in wonder as her strong husband took the tiny pink body into his good arm. She looked so little next to him, but Emma had never seen a more amazing sight. Liam held his daughter as if she were made of glass.

Emma was exhausted, but grateful beyond words for the gift she'd been given. She knew with certainty that things could have turned out much differently than they had. It was a miracle that Leon and Mavis found her when they did. That dear couple had been angels sent from above.

When Daisy began to cry, Liam handed her to Emma, and she placed her daughter at her breast. Instinct kicked in and the baby rooted around until she found her target. For the first time in weeks, Emma relaxed. She and her daughter had been through quite an ordeal. As she looked at her perfect, healthy baby, she knew everything would be fine.

"I was so worried about you." Liam's sat on the edge of the bed next to Emma.

"I know. I didn't think I would ever see you again. I was sure Morgan was going to kill me. I didn't want to hurt her, but I had to. She was behind everything, Liam. I never told you, but I had a run-in with her a couple of months before she came to Beckland. I should have trusted my instincts about her, but I gave her the benefit of the doubt when she pretended to be my friend. You, Jane, and Sadie were all right about her. She was pure evil. She flattened my tires, and she cut your brake lines. She could have killed you, and she tried to kill me. I'm sorry I didn't listen to you."

"Emma, you have the warmest and kindest heart of anyone I've ever known. Don't ever be sorry for that. Morgan used it to her advantage. I should have protected you better." Liam's face looked so pained. "She was out to get you because she was in love with Xavier, and he believes he's in love with you. The jealousy was more than she could take, and she snapped."

"I still don't know what happened to Morgan. Did the police catch her?" Emma had to know the truth.

"Morgan's dead, Emma. She died from the stab wound. She can't ever hurt you again. But considering Xavier's obsession with you, we need to keep a close eye on him." Liam gripped her hand.

Emma let the news sink in. She had mixed feelings about Morgan's death. The woman was deranged, and had every intention of killing Emma. Still, she was conflicted knowing she'd taken a life. It was an issue that would take a long time to work through. Emma knew she'd never be quite the same because of it. But with Daisy safely born, she had more important things that needed her attention.

"I know we have a lot to talk about, but let's put it on the back burner for a while. Tonight, let's just be thankful for our family. I can't wait to introduce Daisy to her sisters."

Emma smiled wearily at Liam, thinking of how excited the girls would be and how she couldn't wait to see them. She missed Sadie too, and wanted to hear how things were going with Colin. If everything between them continued as it had been, they'd have something else to celebrate.

"You're right. Tonight is for happiness, not sadness. You've given me everything I ever wanted, Emma. Look how far we've come. Did you ever think we'd end up here that first day in your coffee shop?" Liam smiled with his lopsided grin and dimple.

"You were relentless. I didn't really have a choice in the matter," Emma chuckled. "One thing is for sure, my life has been a whirlwind since that day. There hasn't been a dull moment since you walked into my life."

"Well, I like to keep things exciting. I wouldn't want you to get bored." Liam ran his hands through his hair and looked at his wife. "The truth is I was so afraid of losing you, Emma."

In less than a year, Emma had met and married the love of her life, been attacked and held hostage in her own home by a psychopath, been stalked and kidnapped by a maniac, and given birth to her fourth child. Her calm and predictable existence had been upended.

Nearly everything she'd been through was life-changing. Most of it was downright traumatic. Some of it would take years to work through. Nevertheless, she wouldn't change a moment of what she'd endured if it meant she and Liam would be together in the end. He and the girls were her entire world, and she'd walk through fire for the opportunity to live the rest of her life with them.

Emma looked into Liam's eyes and saw her own reflection. Their life wasn't perfect. They'd experienced things that most people never did.

When Emma was a little girl, she had visions of a fairy-tale life with Prince Charming. The grown-up Emma knew real life never happened that way.

Love didn't happen that way. Love wasn't pretty. It was heartache, pain, disappointment, and chaos. But when you got it right, it could be the most magical thing in the world. Liam and Emma had created their own special magic, and that was their fairy-tale ending.

Emma clasped her hand in his, knowing she wanted to spend the rest of her life by his side. "You can't get rid of me. It's you and me forever, Liam. For better or for worse."

THIS STORY CONTINUES (AND ENDS) IN *'TIL DEATH DO US PART* (The Vows Book 3).

THANKS

Thanks for reading *For Better or For Worse* (The Vows Trilogy Book 2). I do hope you enjoyed Emma's story. I appreciate your help in spreading the word, including telling a friend. Before you go, it would mean so much to me if you would take a few minutes to write a review and share how you feel about my story so others may find my work. Reviews really do help readers find books. Please leave a review on your favorite book site.

Don't miss out on New Releases, Exclusive Giveaways and much more!

Join my newsletter: http://eepurl.com/cfhMXf
Like me on Facebook: www.facebook.com/heidireneemason
Join my reader group: Heidi's Tribe:
https://www.facebook.com/groups/346156819065335
Follow me on Twitter: @heidireneemason
Follow me on Instagram: @author_heidireneemason
Follow me on BookBub:
https://www.bookbub.com/authors/heidi-renee-mason

Visit my website for my current booklist:
www.heidireneemason.com

I'd love to hear from you directly, too. Please feel free to email me at: heidisbooks999@gmail.com or check out my website www.heidireneemason.com for updates.

ABOUT THE PUBLISHER

Hot Tree Publishing opened its doors in 2015 with an aspiration to bring quality fiction to the world of readers. With the initial focus on romance and a wide spread of romance subgenres, Hot Tree Publishing have since opened their first imprint, Tangled Tree Publishing, specializing in crime, mystery, suspense, and thriller.

Firmly seated in the industry as a leading editing provider to independent authors and small publishing houses, Hot Tree Publishing is the sister company to Hot Tree Editing, founded in 2012. Having established in-house editing and promotions, plus having a well-respected market presence, Hot Tree Publishing endeavors to be a leader in bringing quality stories to the world of readers.

Interested in discovering more amazing reads brought to you by Hot Tree Publishing? Head over to the website for information:

www.hottreepublishing.com